CHANGING TRAINS

Center Point
Large Print

**This Large Print Book carries the
Seal of Approval of N.A.V.H.**

CHANGING TRAINS

CYNTHIA HASELOFF

CENTER POINT LARGE PRINT
THORNDIKE, MAINE

This Center Point Large Print edition
is published in the year 2013 by arrangement with
Golden West Literary Agency.

Special thanks to Jerry Hayes and Danny Jones
for the use of their song, "Changing Trains,"
Copyright © 1993. Used by permission from Negotiable
Publishing, BMI, and General Jones Music, BMI.

The text of this Large Print edition is unabridged.
In other aspects, this book may vary
from the original edition.
Printed in the United States of America
on permanent paper.
Set in 16-point Times New Roman type.

ISBN: 978-1-61173-618-2

Library of Congress Cataloging-in-Publication Data

Haseloff, Cynthia.
 Changing trains / Cynthia Haseloff.
 pages ; cm.
 ISBN 978-1-61173-618-2 (library binding : alk. paper)
 1. Inheritance and succession—Fiction. 2. Indian captivities—Fiction.
   3. Women gamblers—Fiction. 4. Orphans—Fiction.
   5. Large type books. I. Title.
 PS3558.A72294C48 2013
 813′.54—dc23

                                         2012035518

Always For Mama
Who Believed

Special Thanks
to the Railroads

Just after the turn of the 19th Century my maternal grandparents arrived by train in Vernon, Texas during a howling norther. It was very different from the North Carolina and Georgia hills from which they had come. They went by wagon to unsettled land on the withers of the great state where they would build their home and raise their nine children. In time the Doodle Bug, a local of the Katy Railroad, reliably linked that remote outlying settlement to the world beyond. A few miles of track and the vision it excited in men's eyes changed the possibilities for this vast nation.

Our dependence on the railroads is mostly gone. But they remain a present and pleasant memory for my mother and father and others who grew up before super highways and the information highway. The railroads brought the world to them and took them to the world.

Today men like Wally Decker and members of the Katy Railroad Historical Society keep that memory alive. I am indebted to them for the information they provided. Any errors in its presentation or understanding are my own.

Changin' Trains

Comin' to the end of the line,
  But I won't stop now.
Can't waste a moment of time.
  Gonna move on somehow.

Take this weight off my shoulders.
  Take a load off my mind.
Forget the things I told her
  When she left me behind.

Changin' trains.
  Might even change my name.
And I won't look back
  When I change tracks.

People askin' me questions,
  I don't know what to say.
They want to know where I'm goin'.
  Hell, I'm just goin' away.

I never knew what mattered.
  Just went along for the ride.
Now all my dreams have been scattered
  'Cross the countryside.

Changin' trains,
Changin' trains,
Nothing ever stays the same.
Changin' trains,
Changin' trains.

From the song "Changing Trains"
by Jerry Hayes and Danny Jones

Prologue

The Flats, Texas

Light from the smoking chandeliers of the Bee Hive saloon danced off the golden tooth of Flavius Smith as he dealt the last cards around the table. "And one for the lady," he concluded, tossing a card in front of the woman before he laid the deck down.

The stakes were stacked high in the center of the green felt-covered table, with Tim Dawson's winnings for the evening all shoved again into the pot, and matched by the two remaining players. The two men and the woman checked and sorted their hands. Dawson discarded a card. Smith dealt another. The woman, Mari Marshay, considered her hand, but stood pat. Smith looked at her, trying to decide whether she was bluffing already or whether she really held a hand so good she did not need to change it.

"Play cards," grumbled Dawson. "I'll raise another two thousand."

Without a word, Mari Marshay slid a stack of paper money toward the cash piled on the table.

Flavius Smith also added to the pile. "I'll see that, and raise you five thousand."

Dawson's eyes flashed. "That's a mighty big raise for a squirt like you, Flavius. You haven't

11

showed that kind of guts or money all night."

"I never had this hand before. My luck's changing," replied the gambler.

"Maybe you ain't dealt yourself such good luck before," countered the rancher.

The woman listened to the confrontation but took no part. She simply laid $5,000 on the stack.

The rancher, Dawson, shoved his hat back on his head as he studied his hand again. He looked from Flavius Smith to Mari Marshay and back to his hand. His mouth twisted.

"If you are afraid to lose any more . . . ," Smith began.

"I ain't afraid of nothing, you bastard. I've made and lost more money than this bettin' on whether a fly would land on a horse's ass." Dawson's eyes darted toward the woman, but she seemed oblivious to the rough language. Dawson placed his $5,000 in the pot and added another $5,000. "Match that, you worm."

"Certainly," said the mustached gambler. "Are you dropping out, lady?" Mari Marshay placed $5,000 into the growing money stack. Flavius Smith nodded and made his own deposit on the pile of greenbacks and gold. "Five thousand and five more." The gambler casually brushed his cigar onto the floor with his forearm and bent to pick it up, taking his cards with him.

Mari Marshay looked up from her hand as she heard the legs of Tim Dawson's chair screech back on the coarse board floor. Dawson was rising to his feet. "You lowlife, two-bit gambler, keep your hands on the table."

The rancher's hand was already reaching for the pistol at his hip when Flavius Smith reappeared with a gun in his hand. He fired without warning, sending a shot into the chest of the big cattleman. Around the noisy, brawling room, the men at the bar and tables flattened themselves on the floor quickly, overturning tables to get behind anything substantial enough to stop a bullet.

The impact of Smith's slug twisted Dawson to the left, but even then his hand jerked the Colt from its holster and fired it ineffectually at Smith as he fell. He rolled onto his back while Smith watched from the other side of the table. The gambler raised his own weapon with deliberation and eased back on the brass trigger as the dying man on the floor fired one last shot. Dawson's bullet, by intent or accident, hit the gambler squarely in the forehead.

Mari Marshay watched Flavius Smith's shocked face as he crumpled. A dead man's convulsion jerked off a last round into the green table top. The two-bit card cheat hit the floor going back over his chair. One leg dangled lifelessly across the broken rung.

Sheriff Quin Milam was through the door of the Bee Hive at the first shot, the shooting coinciding with his evening rounds. By the second shot, he

13

had surveyed the situation and moved toward it, gun drawn. By the third and fourth, he knew it was too late. He stopped dead still, watching the scene play out before him.

In brief quick bursts the big pistols had thrown a deadly, deafening concussion against the wooden sides of the saloon. In the aftermath the room became silent in that human tribute to mortality and its sudden intrusion into life. An acrid smell settled with the thin blue smoke over the scene as the men waited to see what had happened. The sheriff stared like the others peering out from behind the bar and tables as the woman in the black silk dress rose from her chair and went from Smith to Dawson. Smith was dead, eyes fixed on the open rafters. Mari stepped over the assorted aces that had spilled out of his short boot during the fight. His dead hand still held the cards he had surreptitiously taken. Her manicured fingers gently reached out and rested on the thick artery in Dawson's throat. The sheriff was standing above her when she looked up into his eyes and shook her head. Rising slowly, she casually felt the hole that had followed the bullet through her skirt just below the knee, and then moved back to the table.

"By God, that's the stoniest thing I ever saw . . . sitting through a gunfight like you were at a tea party," swore the marshal. "I never saw anything like that."

14

"Then you have never seen a desperate woman," Marshay answered, pushing the pile of winnings from the table top into the dead rancher's weathered Stetson and tucking it under her arm. In an awkward trembling handshake, she took the marshal's callused hand, leaving several bills in it. "That should cover the funeral expenses," she said calmly.

"Well," the marshal said, shoving the cash into his frayed pocket and studying the bodies at his feet, "that finishes it."

"Yes," agreed the woman in a quiet voice as she looked about the shabby room. "That finishes it."

Before dawn the following morning, as the stage pulled out, it stopped on the outskirts of town to board a passenger, a well-dressed woman. The driver tossed a small, leather-covered trunk, her only luggage, inside as she watched. Mari Marshay never looked back. She climbed into the battered dusty coach, and the driver slapped his reins over the sleek backs of the company mules. Before closing her eyes lightly to sleep away the miles, she leaned back in the seat and placed her slippered foot on the little trunk.

A few days later, Sheriff Milam entered the rented cottage of the lady gambler. Some said she had won close to $100,000, maybe more, the night of the shooting. She had not returned to the gambling hall as usual on subsequent nights. At first this had not seemed unusual since from time to time the lady was known to hold high-stakes games in the small house, following an elegant dinner. But considering the money she had won from Dawson and Smith, the larcenous nature of the town, and the fact that she seldom missed two straight evenings at the Bee Hive, working at her gaming as assiduously as a banker, Milam decided to investigate. The rough lawman felt awkward and self-conscious entering the woman's private domain. He knocked and waited. Gathering himself, he lifted the latch and pushed open the front door of the adobe house. He stood for a moment getting accustomed to the dim light, looking to see if anything was obviously wrong.

"Miss Marshay?" he called out to the emptiness. "Miss Marshay?"

He shyly took in the refined furnishings as he waited just inside the door for any answer that might come. His eyes moved thoughtfully over the room. It was very well kept, nothing amiss, nothing knocked to the floor. When no answer came, Milam stepped down from the tile entry onto the woven rug. His spurs clanked loudly over the tiles as he wandered to the small kitchen. The table was clean with the four matching chairs pushed underneath. The cupboard doors were closed. Inside, a few pounds of flour and corn-meal and some tinned food waited for the next meal. He studied the labels. He smiled slightly at the labeled canned peaches in heavy syrup. His hand hesitated as he turned a tin and read. He had never seen an asparagus. Moving on, he discovered china plates and stemmed glasses. A more mundane service of pottery plates and cups were stacked in the next set of small shelves. There were knives and forks, a lace tablecloth, and napkins in the drawers below.

Closing the last drawer, Milam turned to the center sitting room dominated by an adobe fireplace with raised hearth. A Spanish chest with heavy iron hinges and pulls divided the space informally from the dining area. On it sat a heavy decanter and tumblers of cut glass. Milam removed the crystal stopper and splashed a bit of the amber fire into one of the glasses. He sniffed it, tasted it, and set the glass and its contents back down. It was fine, aged, sipping whisky, not the rotgut the saloon dispensed. Someone who understood whisky and men had chosen it. Opening a polished wood humidor on the chest, he found it full of hand-rolled cigars. Cuban women, they said, rolled them with the sweat from their thighs. Milam closed it and bent to open the front doors of the chest. Inside were several sealed boxes of cards, matches, ashtrays, more cigars, and bottled bourbon. He straightened, wondering who had been the guests at Miss Marshay's evenings of cards, wondering how he had missed this very private gaming among the raucous debauchery of the Western town.

He looked more closely at the room. Miss Marshay could cook and cater to a man in knowing ways, but, he wondered, had there been more than card games going on in the house. He saw no signs of a man in the residence, no hat, no spur, no boot, no shirt discarded. Then his eyes focused on the doorway at the far end of the cottage. There were no doors at the opening, just a pair of heavy curtains that had been drawn back to the sides. The corner of a bed was visible from where he stood. Milam walked heavily toward the portal. Standing with one hand on the adobe facing, he surveyed the room and sighed softly at its pleasantness. He went quickly to the wardrobe and opened the double panels.

The faint smell of lavender and sage drifted into his nostrils. He touched a bundle of sweet grass spiked with the herbs and attached to the door. It was strange to the observant sheriff that a woman of obvious breeding would hang grass like an Indian to freshen her closet. The women he'd known above the town saloons were all devoted to the heavy aromatic fragrances of roses and French water, things that smelled strong and cost money. On the other hand, the woman whose closet he had opened knew how to spend money herself. A half dozen expensive dresses and formal evening gowns had been left hanging inside the big cabinet. Matching shoes sat in a row in front of them. Not a red dress among them, and no sign of a man's familiar company hidden away in the back. Milam closed the doors gently and turned his attention to the rest of the room.

A bright Mexican blanket covered the neatly made bed. An envelope rested against the pillows. Milam stared at it, blinked, then walked quickly to the bed. Hands behind his back, he bent at the waist to read the writing. **Sheriff Quin Milam** was written on the front. For a moment it seemed as if the woman's voice had spoken his name. Straightening, he picked up the letter and opened it.

Sheriff, it began in a clear vertical hand on the engraved personal stationery. **Among the winnings from the fatal game at the Bee Hive was a deed to land on the Clear Fork of the Brazos owned by Mr. Dawson. It is quite a large tract. I do not wish to displace Dawson's widow or children. When you have located them and verified their situation and true claim to the land to my satisfaction, I shall return papers restoring their title to a substantial portion of the property. The rest they may rent or purchase over time at a fair price. Please notify me of the progress of your inquiry.**

You may always reach me through my attorney, Samuel A. Bookman, at 1215 Grande

Avenue, St. Louis, Missouri. A fee for your efforts and inconvenience on my behalf will be sent.

It was signed: **In your debt, Mari Marshay.** Milam smiled slightly even as he frowned over the content. There was a postscript. **Please sell whatever you can of my effects and give the money to someone in need. Or you may hold it as guarantee for your services in expediting the matters with the Dawson heirs.**

Milam touched the paper to his nose, catching a faint fragrance. He carefully folded the note, put it back into the envelope, and dropped it into a large shirt pocket, then patted it in place. Frowning in thought, he surveyed the room. The lady played like a gentleman. It had been a long time since he'd dealt with a gentleman of either sex.

His questing eyes stopped on the small corner fireplace. The noise of his spurs was muffled for a moment as he crossed the thick wool rug. Squatting beside the adobe fireplace, he saw a bit of lace protruding from the ashes inside. Very gently he reached out and picked it up, turning it to the light. Mari Marshay had left everything of value to whoever might find a use for it and had burned her own intimate possessions. He gently stuffed the fragment of lace into his vest pocket.

Outside again, the sheriff stood for a long time on the porch of the house, wiping the sweat from inside his hat with a blue bandanna and gazing down the road that ran away from the lawless Western town. It seemed to him that he had found a shell, a husk, the pale cocoon or shedding of a life outgrown, of the woman who had moved on. The house held for him the same secret knowledge he had felt as a boy discovering a cicada's shell, a tiny connection to a great mystery, an unknown reality. Something was left in the house, something real, something fading, something he had never known and never expected to find among the women he knew. In time he would find the widow Dawson and complete the circle. In time the cottage and its contents would all be broken up and sold as Mari Marshay wished. But for a few moments, as he walked back down the dusty street toward his dingy office and hard bunk, he considered keeping the cottage just as he had kept the cicada's shell on his window sill until it became dust.

Chapter One

Denison, Texas

The Missouri, Kansas, and Texas beat the Border Tier Railway to Indian Territory at Chetopa, Kansas on June 6, 1870. There was a celebration. A commemorative forty-five pound rail, brought at great expense from Sheffield, England, was laid across the border. The brand-new, little, wood-burning Grant 4-4-0 engine with its very important passengers then steamed across. After that, there were free rides out to Russell Creek and back for the townsfolk, and plenty of fireworks and firewater.

The railroad men called the Indian Territory the "Indian Bridge," seeing it only as a slender iron means of transit from Kansas to Texas. They did not expect to receive their usual ten sections of land per mile on either side of the unfurling rails to sell to immigrants. This land still belonged to the Indians in 1870. The white man had not yet found the legal means to divest them of their communal, tribal property.

Crossing the "bridge" took the M.K.&T. until Christmas night, 1872—taking thirty months to lay the rail from Junction City, Kansas to Denison, Texas. Sometimes the Irish Brigade laid five miles of track in a day. Mostly they were good for a mile a day, not counting surveying, grading, and bridge building, heat, rain, and northers. But they were not pushing to beat the Border Tier then. They were just methodically, mile by mile, opening the last frontier, a small dark enclave hidden in the very heart of the country.

At Denison, Texas, the Katy, as the M.K.&T. Railroad became affectionately known, came to a stop, waiting to join the Houston and Texas Central, waiting to link the country again north and south, west of the Mississippi. End of tracks was all the hope and joy and degradation and disaster a human being could stand.

By the time the Houston & Texas Central reached Denison three months later, in March of 1873, the town was thriving. Hanna and Owens, commissary men to the railroaders, had set up their grocery headquarters in a permanent location. The Overland Transit Company with its enormous wagon yards and prairie ships hauled heavy freight delivered to the railhead from St. Louis to points beyond. The shacks and houses from Red River City, Sherman, Preston, Warren, and Carpenter's Bluff had come across the baked land over the dust-dry or mud-deep roads on rollers. A city had appeared almost overnight. There was a school and even a church.

The terminus of the railroad spread out for miles. White tents stretched out in the Texas sun.

Around the Katy's army of tracklayers, tie men, and gandy dancers, the immigrants pitched their camps, clinging to the iron men in the dangerous new land.

A block south of Main Street, the notorious Sazerac and its compatriot saloons waited for the iron men to be paid. They catered to the men in their weaknesses. Millie Hipps and her doves from Mollie Andrew's establishment in Sedalia, Missouri entertained the high-class trade. The Irish and Indian and Mexican and Negro girls made do along Skiddy Street, a cleared-out ravine lined on both sides with every manner of tent, shack, and wood or cloth structure that would keep out rain and keep in a minuscule privacy.

"Watch the go'-damn barrel, ye idiot!" the freight driver shouted to the thickly muscled loader. "Move it, now. I ain't got all day, ye churl!" He tipped his hat briefly to the heavily perfumed, satin-clad beauty that walked past without a glance at him. "Aye, there's a refreshing sight to a needy man. Like cold beer on a hot day," he said to himself. "Quit gappin', ye peckerwoods!" he shouted at the freight hands who slowed in appreciation of the harlot. "This ain't no dovecote for languid looks and lascivious thoughts." He watched longingly as the exotic woman disappeared in the crowd.

"Excuse me, sir," Mrs. Todd spoke with a crisp

tone. "I am trying to get to the ticket window there. You are blockin' my way with your ooglin'."

The freight driver replaced his hat and stepped aside. Mrs. Todd proceeded. She was a small woman, well into middle age, clad in the garments of a widow. A black woman followed her closely.

"Ooglin', indeed! Holy Mother of God, but an honest woman dries up a man's juices." The teamster spat off the dock onto the dirt beside the track. "Hurry up, boys. I'm tirin' meself here in the sun, meltin' me sweet Irish heart."

Farther down the platform another pair of eyes observed the prostitute walking toward the train. Boudinot, the Indian lawyer, casually watched the blue eyes that followed her. "Keep your mind off women. A mistake here could get you killed."

"I like women, Brother, and they like me," the younger man said. "It's a family trait, isn't it?"

The conversation between the men was carried on as if they were strangers, men who happened to stand beside each other not really seeing each other as they waited to go to their destinations. "Keep your mind off women. Stay in the immigrant car and don't call attention to yourself. If we can get you back to Three Forks *alive,* I'll be able to work out something with the railroad. But not here. Not in Texas."

"Whoo, she's prime meat," answered the younger man, cocking his head better to take in the view of the woman. He did not seem to hear his brother's instructions. "I like 'em big and mean . . . and not too smart. A good brain has ruined many an appetizing woman. She's passing your car, Brother. Maybe she'll stop by mine."

Boudinot sighed. "Watie, don't take chances. This can be worked. I can do it."

"I'm not going to prison," Watie Boudinot said, and walked away toward the immigrant cars behind the satin-clad woman, late of the Sazerac. He followed her closely, watching the shapely behind. When she turned, he smiled brightly, wrapped an arm around her, and drew her between the immigrant cars. Looking back, he threw a grin toward his brother.

Mrs. Todd stopped at the small ticket window. "I'm goin' to Saint Louis, first-class ticket, president's special," she said. "My son left the two tickets . . . for Missus Omar Todd and her maid."

The clerk rustled around in the hidden recesses of his cage unimpressed by the name of the late Union officer or his bride. He shoved the tickets through the iron bars. "One way," he said flatly.

"Well, of course." The little woman observed the clerk. "I'm already here, am I not? Had my visit." Mrs. Todd backed up to thrust the tickets into her purse, driving her elbow into the stomach of the Reverend John Beecher.

26

"Please, madam," he spluttered.

Mrs. Todd glared at him, then she started to the train, insistently pushing her way through the freight and boarding immigrants, through the hawkers, candy boys, and swindlers, through the soldiers and Indians of a dozen once mighty nations, through the hurried, heedless world that had replaced her own. "Rush, rush, rush, Louisey," she said to her maid, following at a respectable distance. "Everybody's pushing about these days. Not like it used to be when people had a proper concept of their place and respect for their betters. Look at these vagabonds. The war changed everything, and not altogether for the better, I think."

"Yes'am," agreed the Negro woman carrying Mrs. Todd's vanity case, shoving through the riff-raff with abandon. "Life shore is a bitch down amongst the folkses." Something in the black woman's tone caused Mrs. Todd to pause on the iron step and look at her critically. Louisey smiled brightly, and Mrs. Todd went inside the dark green coach.

The freight driver, Clancy, dropped off the platform to check the load on his wagon. Standing on the ground beside it, he turned back to the dockhands that had suddenly stopped, still holding their heavy boxes. "What the hell is slowing ye down now . . . ?" Clancy started to

27

say. His eyes fell dead level on the slender, silk-clad ankle. "I've died," he whispered as his eyes continued up the line of this new woman's body.

Clancy vaulted to the platform to stand with the other men as the woman continued toward the train through the milling multitude. A black child with an umbrella under his arm and a small cart of bags and boxes followed her. Clancy's callused hand fell on the boy's shoulder as he passed, keeping him from blocking his view. The child looked up into the tanned, unshaven face. Clancy patted his shoulder absently, intent on the woman.

"Where'd she come from, son?" he asked.

"Off the San Antone stage, mister," the boy answered.

Clancy held him until the woman moved into the dense throng and finally handed her ticket to the conductor. Standing on the step of the train car christened *The Prairie Queen*, she turned to survey the scene and search for her luggage while he checked the ticket. Clancy released the boy and tipped his hat as the lady's eyes found him.

"There's an angel if ever I seen one," Clancy said as the woman nodded slowly, then entered the train slowly. "An angel."

"That ain't no angel," one of the freight hands said, dropping his box heavily onto the wagon. "That's The Pagan, The Pagan Rose . . . beautiful

28

to look at, deadly to touch. She's ruined more men than the potato blight. I seen her before in San Antone."

"You was drinkin'," Clancy said skeptically.

"No. I's sober as a judge," replied the hand. "I seen her close. She's smokin' a little cigar and puttin' a wad of cash big enough to choke that mule in her little purse."

"Whore don't make that kind of money," observed Clancy.

"She ain't no whore. She ain't even know to dally. She's a gambler," the other man muttered. "A damn' woman high-stakes gambler. Cleaned the house with three jacks."

Clancy smiled. "That's even better. A lady what pays her own way. She got a real name?"

"Mari Madeline Marshay," answered the loading hand. "Prettier than Pagan, ain't it?"

"Much prettier," agreed Clancy. "But Pagan . . . ah, there's a name for contemplation."

Chapter Two

A group of cavalry officers strolled past the freight being loaded. "There's Captain Howard," one said. He stuck up his hand, signaling a man leaning idly out of one of the train's special car windows, watching the scenes unfolding along the platform without much interest. The soldiers dodged around a pile of baggage and an immigrant family struggling to stay together and make their way to their car.

"All ready, eh?" asked one of the officers outside the train.

"That's right," answered Captain Phillip Howard. Howard wore the studied air of nonchalance cultivated by men of wealth and refinement on the frontier. "All ready."

A small man in a priest's garments bowed to the American officers as he passed along the train side toward the engine. They received and returned his courtesy and watched as he waited to climb aboard behind a man being lifted into an elegant wheelchair. The invalid's face and form were hidden beneath a heavy wrapping of coat and shawl and a fur hat on his head, strange protection against the drafts of summer travel. His gloved hands struck out at the black man who sat him in the chair.

"Clumsy black bastard!" the invalid shouted, and let himself be wheeled into the car.

"Your patient?" asked the major below Howard's window.

"Not mine," said Phillip Howard, shaking his head.

The compartments in the railroad's elegantly appointed special passenger car were small, with a light pecan paneling and tufted green leather chairs that swiveled on floor mounts beside the windows. Ottomans sat within easy reach. Near the compartments on either end of the long interior were small lavatories. A hand-painted water basin and pitcher were also available in each cubicle. A barber chair and shaving equipment occupied an area near the last, larger, master compartment. The car itself was built on the new Pullman design and was longer, higher, and wider than the first 1859 model. The aisle walls of the private cubicles contained sliding doors. The design of etched glass above ornately carved wood panels depicted prairie scenes. Divider walls between the few rooms of the main car carried pull-down beds for sleeping and bench type seats for day riding. The latter could also be used as a second bed. A spacious lounge equipped with more plush seating, tables for writing and cards, a small library, and a bar occupied the center of the car. It was equipped with a tile stove for winter travel or at least for atmosphere during winter travel. As all the new

Pullman coaches, the car was really heated by a hot air furnace under the floor. It was ventilated through the deck windows. The motif of Western scenes ran throughout the carved paneling, accentuated by leather furniture, brass and glass lamps, and other appointments. A George Catlin painting of a regal Kiowa woman held court over the lounge. The railway president had spared no expense. The car was, after all, called *The Prairie Queen.*

Mari Marshay entered her compartment behind the black child. She walked to the window, glanced at the view before her, and pulled down the shade against the glaring sun while the boy stacked her things neatly on the floor. As he finished, her eyes sought the small leather trunk among the new luggage. She smiled at the boy and handed him a silver dollar.

"Thank you, missy," the boy exclaimed, backing out the door. "Thank you."

"Porter!" the Reverend John Beecher called out from the window nearest the steps. "Porter, come in here at once! This is disgraceful . . . right here in the middle of the day. No effort whatsoever to conceal their . . . their . . ."

"Excuse me, sir," the porter said, as he tried to ease by a large, heavy-bodied man standing on the train's iron boarding steps. The man, Boudinot, shoved him back, observed him with cold blue eyes, and entered the train deliberately and without haste.

"Bit like looking in the neighbor's windows, eh?" one of the officers noted.

Unnoticed by the soldiers fixed on Boudinot's hostile behavior, a slender young girl gently helped a tall man clad in fringed and beaded buckskins up the steps. The old trapper's large gnarled hand grasped the girl's thin shoulder tightly as he leaned heavily on her, his fragile security in an unknown world, a world left behind fifty years before.

By the time the porter reached Reverend Beecher, he was walking the aisle impatiently.

"There are innocent women and children all along this train forced to observe that." He pointed out the window without looking at Watie Boudinot and the prostitute entwined against the side of a small building.

The porter looked stunned for a moment. "What can I do, sir? There's a little dog in all of us."

"Not all of us," growled Beecher. "And certainly not in public. Good God in heaven, this is a civilized country, not Hai-i-ti or some other primitive outpost."

The porter continued to watch out the window. "They're finishin' up, sir, buttonin' up. Be movin' right along as soon as she's paid." He straightened and pulled down the shade. "You can go in now without danger of further offense."

Beecher glowered at the porter. "You've been a great help," he muttered sarcastically.

Outside, on the boarding side of the train, one of Howard's officer friends inquired: "Don't need anything from one of the news hawks to read, nothing like that?"

Howard revealed a book held in his hand to the man outside the train. "Good book to pass the time. Nice of you men to see me off."

"Guess you'll be bored soon enough," continued the major. "Good to have the book."

"Not so bored," interrupted an aging lieutenant. "I think I saw The Pagan come on board."

"The Pagan?" asked Captain Howard without enthusiasm.

"That's right, old scout, The Pagan . . . a notorious woman of the Texas frontier. A lady ruined somewhere. They say she shed her faith in God and man. She's ruined a hundred men in return. Takes no prisoners, so to speak . . . a beautiful barbarian just like her ancestors that emerged from the deep forests of the old world to destroy civilization . . . a pagan."

"Poet are you, Baxter? As I recall, it was the barbarians who were changed by the faith." Howard spoke without much interest in the woman. "Really, how rare is another whore in Texas?"

Lieutenant Baxter did not reply, but his eyes

like Howard's followed the signalman toward the engine. The others also noted the preparation for impending departure.

"Looks like you're getting off at last," Baxter said uncomfortably. "Give our regards to civilization, then."

"That's right," agreed the major. "Have a good trip, Captain."

The soldiers backed away from the train. Howard gave them a slight wave as they disappeared into the crowd. Relieved of their gentlemanly duty, the men were eager for their leave in the dens of Denison.

"Boy!" Mrs. Todd called to a passing news hawk from the window near Howard. "This paper you sold me is old. I already read about that fire in Chicago in October! Even the children are crooks," she commented, turning toward Captain Howard. He shrugged, and she turned to the man at the other window beside her. "Well?"

As the woman withdrew to the aisle in pursuit of the news hawk, the man at the window, known as Joe Crites, muttered to himself: "The old girl ought to keep it. Anything new would just confuse her."

Leaning against an awning support post, Denison's town marshal, Lee Hall, took in the scene before him. The sprawl, the confusion, the chaos somehow resolved itself as each traveler scurried to his destination. Each knew only his own interest and remained oblivious to the greater purposes unfolding—opening the continent, changing the world for good and bad forever. Hall shifted the toothpick in his teeth. He was detached from the plans and purposes of the travelers, yet watching carefully in his apparent somnambulism. His eyes ran over the boarding immigrants quickly, over the crowd of young hawkers working through the crowd. From time to time, he'd had to chasten these boys who sold food and other necessities to the passengers. Sometimes their greed got out of hand, and they did not provide the goods or services for the dollars received. Just kids, the hawkers could make more money than the engineer could if they were good businessmen. They were everywhere. They saw everything.

Hall spotted Jimmy Wing. He smiled, thinking about the tough, salty kid. Couldn't be more than fourteen and already supporting his mother and three sisters and looking for the next step up. Wing worked his way along the train toward the president's car – a rolling palace owned by the railroad's top man and used primarily for his business and personal needs, and for special guests. Hall already knew why the car was attached. It had arrived the night before and had been placed on a siding awaiting its privileged passengers. One in particular was mighty important to the line president, Alfred Huxley. Wing disappeared into an immigrant car. In a little while he emerged at the rear door. His tray looked nearly empty. He began selling to the crowd as he worked his way back toward the station and his cache of supplies. By the time he reached Hall, only a sandwich and an orange remained.

"What say, Marshal?" the kid asked. "Buy my last sandwich, and I'll toss in the orange and talk a minute."

Marshal Hall lifted the sandwich from the tray and looked at it. **Roast beef** was written in pencil on the brown wrapping paper. "Your mother still make these, Jimmy?"

Wing nodded. "That's bread baked this morning, and that's the best beef in Texas."

The marshal reached into his vest pocket and handed over the required coins.

Jimmy Wing stashed the money and picked up the orange. He tossed it in the air and caught it a couple of times as the marshal unwrapped his sandwich and took a bite.

He spoke with his mouth full. "Well, Jim, let's hear it."

Wing continued to toss the orange as he turned about to check the crowd. "There's a passenger with the immigrants that don't exactly fit. He ain't makin' no show, and he's sitting in a dark corner. I figure he don't want to be seen, maybe. Looks kinda like a Injun to me."

"Lots of Indians ride the train," chewed the marshal. "Maybe he's a shy man . . . or just ashamed riding the cheap cars with the foreigners."

"Yeah. Maybe so." Jimmy Wing tossed the orange to Hall who caught it with his left hand. "I'll be workin' the other cars and see what's happening." Leaving the lawman, the boy went into the dépôt to refill his tray of food. Lee Hall wiped his red mustache and beard as he wadded the empty sandwich paper and tossed it into an overflowing trashcan.

Chapter Three

Joe Crites still hung in the passenger car window, getting air, watching the bustling scene intently. "I'll lay you ten to one we don't get to Saint Louis on time," he wagered with the dark man at the window beside his.

"We are crossing the Nations," Boudinot replied in a soft, articulate voice. "You might just be lucky to get to Saint Louis, at all." He smiled to himself.

"You've ridden *The Prairie Queen* before, then?" pursued Crites.

"Several times," the man answered, continuing to look at the throng seething before them around the train.

Crites offered his hand across the support post. "Joe Crites," he said. "I bet on what will and what won't, what can and what can't. Anything interests me, but land speculation is my business. Lots of speculation in Texas. I've heard there can be trouble on this train."

The other man ignored his words, but accepted his hand with a solid shake. "Boudinot."

" 'Board," called out the conductor, the earnest captain of the train crew. "Let's go, folks. *All aboard!* Boarding now for McAlester, Parson City, Saint Louis, Chicago, and all points east." He turned and shouted one last time: *"All abooaard!"*

The conductor swung up on the step at the front of the car to check the fore and aft situations. Satisfied, he signaled the engine. The first released pressure shifted back through the cars. A slight jolt breaking inertia lifted the languid *Prairie Queen* from her glistening couch. She coughed deeply, and eased onto her knees. Ringing the bell languidly, the stoker warned the bystanders away from the moving train. The crowd along the tracks migrated back away from her. The big iron wheels grasped the rails as the engine blew steam into the retreating throng. The terminal began to inch back as the *Queen* crept forward.

Jimmy Wing stopped briefly beside Marshal Hall. "Got to catch up with my merchandise," he said quickly. "But I saw something interesting in the president's car. Boudinot is back there. Boudinot looks a lot like the man in the immigrant car."

Hall straightened. "You think that man is his baby brother, Watie?"

"Could be." The boy skipped away backwards toward the train. "There's a good reward from the railroad for that little robbery he pulled over at Limestone Gap. Ain't that cute . . . robbin' trains and then ridin' 'em back home? Anyhow, a telegram to Fort Smith might get some law out to McAlester for a look-see. Wouldn't hurt to check it out. Don't forget who told you. My ma could use the reward."

40

As quickly as he had appeared, Jimmy Wing was off after the train. Hall drew deeply on his pipe. The town marshal walked thoughtfully with his head down and hands clasped behind his back toward the station and its telegrapher. *The Prairie Queen* rolled slowly out of Denison.

"Well, we're off on time." Crites nodded to Boudinot as the train began to move along.

The *Queen* began a crawl over the glittering iron into the open, a step, two steps, a few more, and then the whistle shrieked. She sighed and slipped back to a halt.

"What's wrong now?" spluttered Reverend John Beecher, trying to see over Crites's shoulder.

"You're entering a different world here," said Boudinot stoically. "In the Nations time and life have no value."

Crites leaned farther out, watching the trainmen scurrying forward. "Longhorns! A herd of cattle right across the damn' tracks." A cowboy on horseback dashed forward along the side of the cars. "Texas," Crites whispered in soft disgust. "Me, I like Chicago where the beef is on a plate."

Resting on his elbow at a window, Captain Howard watched the efforts to move the herd. He finally turned toward the rear of the car.

Outside, cowboys shouted and galloped forward

41

on their tough little ponies. One of the cowboys whirled his nag, taking in the woman in the window in front of him. He swept off his hat in a gallant salute. "Take care of my money, honey," he shouted with a smile, and rode away.

Howard's attention focused on the woman. The sight of her caused him to straighten.

"Mari?" he whispered.

The woman turned slowly from the window, smiled slightly. "Well, Doc, it's been a long time." She offered her hand across the partition. Captain Howard took it and held it. "Maybe I should be more respectful after so much time?" She gently withdrew her hand from Howard's firm, lingering grasp.

"You were never respectful, my dear. You always called me Doc." He studied his hands, the cover of the book he held. "I never thought we'd meet again."

The woman's smile broadened. "You never know what to expect on a train. Modern technology and the vicissitudes of travel combine to make life twice as interesting. You're staring, Doc."

"Sorry, Mari, I guess I'm still shocked to see you."

"Have I lost my looks?" A humorous twinkle in the eyes and wry smile flickered over Mari's face.

"No." Howard studied her closely. "You're more beautiful than ever. But somehow you are different."

Mari's eyes wandered to the floor. "I'm not a little girl any more. I'm older, wiser."

"Never married?"

"No, but I have another name, Doc," Mari answered, looking directly into Howard's eyes. "Before you wander too far down the path of fond memories, you should know I'm called The Pagan now."

"So you're The Pagan?" He paused. "Then . . . that's what the cowboy meant about his money!" The words hissed from Howard's tight lips.

"It was a fair fight, Doc. I didn't take anything he couldn't afford to lose." Mari watched Howard turn away, only his shoulder and profile remaining visible to her. "So, Doc, after all this time you are still quick to believe everything bad you hear about me."

"That's right. I haven't changed." Howard continued looking away from the woman. "I haven't changed at all. I will never accept your games. Good to see you again."

Mari observed the sudden coldness. She turned and started toward her compartment, then stopped briefly. "Everybody changes, Doc. I just realized how much I have changed. Seeing you again after all this time, my heart didn't stop like I once thought it would. I can finally say something I never thought I could. I don't love you any more, Doc. I'm sure that is as much a relief to you as to me. Good bye."

Howard turned and watched the woman walk away. His face showed nothing of the unexpected pain the words had brought. He heard them again and again repeating softly: *I don't love you any more, Doc.*

"Well, that's settled, then," Phillip Howard muttered to himself as he leaned back over the windowsill. His mind asked without hesitation: *Is it?*

The engineer pulled the whistle in short bursts as the last of the Texas cattle were cleared from the tracks. Howard observed the engineer as he waved to the cowboy on drag, the one who had spoken familiarly to Mari Marshay. The doctor bristled at the impudence. He carefully considered the romantic figure in leather chaps and broad-brimmed hat with a bright silk scarf tied at his throat. Could a woman of intelligence really take an interest in such a man—a man with nothing to offer but bravado, a man with no future but hardship? Had Mari lowered herself to being accosted at train windows by cowboys? The doctor shrugged cynically. The mind of a woman was a mystery, but the railroad he understood. Cows were big business to the Katy, money in the pockets of the railroads and the packers. There was no gain in offending paying customers, even cowboys. The engineer released the brake and eased the throttle gently forward.

Starting back toward his compartment, Howard

bumped against the wall as, at last, *The Prairie Queen* inched forward again. She was fully awake now, moving with purpose toward the Red River Bridge, toward the dark and unknown Nations, a land of thickly shadowed sunlight where things were rarely what they seemed.

Chapter Four

San Antonio, Texas

"I'm trying to find a woman who came through here about a week ago? Maybe five and a half feet tall, slim, blonde, nice clothes, refined. Handsome woman, easy for a man to remember." Sheriff Quin Milam addressed the dépôt agent. "She'd've come from The Flats. Didn't have much luggage."

The San Antonio stage agent observed the badge on the man's shirt. "Lots of folks come through here . . . even some good-looking women, now and then. She wanted for something?" he asked suspiciously.

"No," replied Milam. "Near as I can tell, she's an honest woman. But she's come into some property out on the Brazos, and there's a problem about one of the heirs. I think she'd want to handle it herself. I imagine she would stay over here a spell, rest up, buy some clothes maybe, then move on, maybe Saint Louis. That's the address of the lawyer she gave me."

"She gave you an address?" The stage master considered Quin Milam closely. "Which side you fight for, sir?"

"I rode with John Bell Hood and got my ass whupped," replied Milam.

46

"Officer?"

"Captain . . . which will buy you a glass of beer on a hot day with the right amount of coin."

The stage agent inhaled deeply but stood a bit more erect. "My two brothers died at the Bloody Angle."

There was a brief pause, nothing to be said by either man.

"Miss Marshay arrived a little over a week ago," said the agent. "Stays with Mister and Missus Gustav von Trauben in the King Wilhelm District, when she's in town. They're richer than a foot up a bull's butt. She left yesterday morning for Denison to catch the train to Saint Louis."

"Well, I'll be damned." Milam smiled. "That was easy, even if she's moved on."

"Not so easy, Sheriff, if you are playing this false. Miss Marshay is well respected by powerful people in San Antone. She's a lady. You'd best remember that." The agent returned to his work.

Milam felt some irritation at the implied accusation. "Well, I didn't think she was a barfly. I'll need a ticket on the Denison stage. The kid rides free?"

The agent saw the child then—a little girl, about four. If he wondered why a sheriff in pursuit of a woman had a child with him, he did not show it. "She'll have to sit in your lap if the stage is crowded. And it's always crowded."

47

Milam nodded, laid down his money, and took the ticket when it was ready. "Next stage leaves at five o'clock this evening. Cooler then, easier on the men and horses. There's a good place to eat across the street and a beer garden a couple of blocks over. Beer's good. Food's stout. It's not a saloon. Germans don't mind you bringing a child in there. Their wives and kids are all around the place." The agent thought a minute. "Ain't American. No fighting or whoring." As he looked down, he added: "She'll be gone by the time you reach Denison."

"Don't matter," the lawman said, walking away with the child's hand in his. "I just keep a-comin'."

Milam was only a day behind Mari Marshay as he placed the little girl into the stage and climbed aboard himself, making it sway with his weight. He directed the girl out of his way, sat heavily, contentedly, and lifted her onto his lap. She toyed with the badge on his shirt.

"Your little girl is cute, Sheriff," observed the portly woman passenger whose broad hips crowded his own.

"She ain't my child, ma'am." He could not bring himself to say the word orphan about the little girl he'd brought with him.

"Prisoner?" The woman chuckled.

"I'm delivering her to someone," Milam said

affably. Yes, he thought, that was what he was doing. It was that simple. It had begun very simply, this journey—perhaps not so simply. In the beginning, there was more in the way of desperation until he'd remembered the letter.

Sheriff Quin Milam sighed over the ledger book on his desk. He seemed too large for the high stool where he sat with one boot heel hooked over a rung and the other leg stretched straight out. His large hands held the pencil he had just sharpened with his pocketknife. The door opened. Milam looked up gratefully.

"Sheriff," the voice of Digger Charles spoke quietly in the professional voice he used as the town undertaker.

"Come on in, Digger," Milam said amiably. "You don't have to slither around here in deference to the dead. Come right in. Speak right up."

As the gaunt man entered, Milam returned his attention to the big open book on his high desk.

The undertaker came to a stop in front of the sheriff. "How are you, Sheriff?"

Milam closed the book. "My life is a continual feast, Digger. How're you doin'?"

"Well, Quin," he began, "I have a problem."

Problems weren't unexpected by the sheriff. They were, after all, why he was in business.

49

"What sort of a problem?" Digger Charles pursed his lips and looked down. "Speak up, Digger. Ain't nobody died violently since that shoot-out at the Bee Hive. You've been paid for that, and got 'em planted."

The undertaker cleared his throat and, capturing Milam's eye, looked meaningfully down again.

"Good God, Digger, what's so mysterious?" Milam rose from his stool to peer over the desk to where the other man pointed with his gaze. He looked back at the black-clad mortician. "It's a kid."

"No," Digger Charles said. "It's Tim Dawson's kid."

"Well?"

"Well, she's been at my place for three days, and nobody's claimed her. Fritz brought her over from the hotel for the funeral, and he never came back to get her. My wife is not a robust woman, and doesn't know what to do with her. We've decided to turn her over to you to deliver . . . wherever."

"Where's her mother?"

"I don't know that. Fritz just brought her and her father's kit over from the hotel and left her. I have to lay out Mother Weaver now, Quin. The kid's your problem. You stay with him now," he admonished the child, and turned on his polished heel to depart the dingy office.

Quin rose again on the stool to look over the desk. The little girl waited quietly. Her hair was black and not too clean and neither were her clothes, the tattered remnants of a dress and moccasins. She looked up into his face. The sheriff sighed and got down from the stool. He walked around and stood with hands on hips, looking at the waif. The child shivered visibly, but did not retreat from the towering man.

"What's your name?" Milam's voice suddenly sounded loud and rough to him. He grimaced. The child's eyes fixed innocently on him. "What's your name, little girl?" Milam squatted over his spurs. "Do you have a name?"

"Cricket," the child whispered, studying Milam's face.

"Cricket's a bug," Milam said. "Is that your name?" The child nodded. "Cricket Dawson?" The child did not nod again. "What was your father's name?"

The little girl blinked. "Pa."

"Where's your ma?" The child's eyes were bright and alert, but she did not respond to his question. "You got a ma?"

"No," she said without regret.

Milam looked down at the floor as he thought. The girl bent her head to see his face. "Well, Cricket, I guess I'd better go see Fritz at the hotel. I'll get Maudy at the café to watch after you."

Cricket Dawson walked beside Sheriff Quin Milam down the board sidewalk. He slowed his long strides to accommodate her little ones. The café was three doors down, not so far. Milam saw it as a hope, a place to leave the girl with the amiable and well-built mother of the cowboys and drifters of the rowdy town. He opened the door in to the midst of the crowded room, searching for Maudy through the pushing and shoving and reaching bodies of the diners.

"Well, Quin," a voice behind him said. "There ain't a table left. You can wait, or I can send Pedro down to your office with a tray when the bustle clears out."

"Maudy, I need your help," stammered Milam.

"Not right now, sweetie." Maudy started off with a load of dishes.

Milam caught her arm. "No, Maudy, I need your help."

Maudy turned, holding the plates, to analyze the sheriff's face. "So, shoot." Milam looked down. Maudy cocked her head. "So?"

"Down there." Milam pointed shyly.

Maudy looked down. "Well, it's a kid, Quin." She turned to the crowded house and shouted: "Anybody here lose a little girl?"

"She ain't lost," said Milam. "I need to leave her with you." The child slipped her little hand into Milam's.

Maudy just laughed in Quin Milam's face. She laughed all the way back to the kitchen, dodging through the mass of chairs and elbows and hungry men along the way.

"Come on, then." Milam gripped Cricket's hand and opened the door.

The only real hotel in The Flats was on the other side of the wide, rutted street. He started down the steps and out into the traffic. The child stumbled over the coarse ground. Milam rescued her from a fall, pulling her up by her frail arm. As he looked down, a teamster yelled out: "I ain't got all day, Dad-dy."

"Move your ass then, you son-of-a-bitch, before I throw it in jail!" Milam shouted back, trying to regain his authority. He lifted the little girl into his arms and crossed the street. She rode easily, putting an arm around his neck, taking in the scenery as if accustomed to the vantage point. Milam smiled at her.

They entered the hotel and approached the front desk where Fritz was dusting, a useless and unrewarding task. "Hey, little girl," Fritz said. "How you doin', peaches?"

"She ain't doin' too damn' good," Milam responded for her. "Digger Charles booted her out of the undertaking parlor and gave her to me. I'm trying to find out where she belongs."

"Well, she don't belong here," Fritz answered suspiciously. "Tim Dawson bought a room. That's all I know."

"Oh, you know more than that, Fritz," stated Milam. "You know just about everything there is to know."

"I don't know nothing about the kid. After Dawson was killed, I went up to clean out the room. She was asleep right where he left her when he went out to play cards. I took her and his effects over to the undertaker. That's all I could do."

"Where's her mother?"

"Dawson came in by himself with the little girl." The clerk's mouth was set tightly.

"And . . . ?"

Fritz polished the wood harder. "I don't think there is a mother . . . not with him, anyway."

Milam scrutinized the clerk.

"First thing he did after putting the child in the room was look up Pearl Blaine. Pearl would maybe know something."

"Thank you, for your assistance, Fritz." Milam's voice showed some sarcasm. "Well, I ain't takin' this little girl into Pearl's establishment." He sat Cricket Dawson gently on the counter. "You watch her," he directed

Fritz, and walked toward the swinging doors that separated the hotel lobby from the saloon and its celebrated vices.

"If it ain't the darlin' sheriff." Pearl Blaine smiled and cocked her leg on the table where she sat. "Let you see the little birdy on my knee for four bits." She hiked her skirt up, revealing a portion of a bright tattoo. "Let you play in the nest for a dollar."

"You just get that?" Milam asked curiously, then recovered. "Don't waste that on me, Pearl. Save it for the cowboys and kids." He sat down so that he could look through the swinging doors to where Cricket sat on the desk.

Pearl slid her hand along his thigh. "What you want, Sheriff, honey?"

Milam put her hand back on the table and held it there until Pearl grasped his intent fully. "I want to know what you know about Tim Dawson."

"He was killed in a card game with that woman gambler, The Pagan. She didn't shoot him. Flavius Smith did. They killed each other on the spot . . . Flavius and Dawson. I was upstairs, so I didn't see it, but that's what I hear happened." Pearl was now interested in her fingernails since the potential buyer had disqualified himself.

"I knows he's dead," said Milam. "I want to know how he lived before he died."

Pearl looked into the sheriff's eyes. "He was a real sweet man. Nothin' rough or peculiar. Just liked to do it, then lay there a while and talk."

"What did he talk about, Pearl?"

"Well . . ." The prostitute thought a few moments. "He was real sad, had a hard life. He married a woman a lot younger than he was, and it looked like they was goin' to be real happy. But she had a baby and died. He done the best he could with the kid, way out on his ranch . . . found a wet nurse who raised her up some till she moved on. Shoot, a man don't know nothing about kids, ex-specially girls. The child was a girl."

"Did the mother have any family?"

"Shoot, Sheriff, he said he found her walking down the road, just a little old runned-off girl herself. Felt sorry for her and took her in. He needed a cook and house-keeper. She needed a place to live. Then later they got married. His wife was always saying God would look out for them, but I guess she was wrong. He'd come to town to sell his ranch so he could take the little girl to San Antone and live there. That'd be a better place for his little girl, what with schools and all. But he couldn't sell that damn' ranch."

"No," said the sheriff thoughtfully. "He used it for a stake in a poker game, instead."

Milam heard the scream from the hotel lobby and the wails of the child in pain. He jumped up from his chair, leaving poor Pearl to ponder the melancholy state of mankind. He found Cricket lying on the floor with Fritz trying to pick her up as she kicked and screamed.

He pushed Fritz aside and lifted the crying child. "God Almighty, Fritz! What the hell did you do?"

"I didn't do nothin'," protested the rattled clerk. "She fell off backwards."

"Shit," murmured Quin Milam as he gently tossed the child in his arms. Walking away, he pulled out the big blue bandanna from his pocket and began to wipe the tears from her cheeks. He whispered soft sympathy to the orphan in his arms, pulling her tiny hand from the lump rising on the back of her head as he examined it.

Returning to his office, he held the child until she fell asleep in his arms, then he laid her on the bunk in the cell he used as his bedchamber. He could hear her breathing softly as he sat down at his desk. His thoughts drifted.

"So what'd you do with the little girl?" Maudy asked as she backed through the door with a big tray of food.

Quin put his finger to his lips, then pointed

at the cell. Maudy set the tray down quietly, and returned to close the door.

"Well?" she asked as she began to uncover the tray.

Milam accepted a napkin and tucked it into his collar. "I don't know. Fritz says there was no woman with Dawson. Pearl Blaine says his wife died, leaving him with the child. Says his wife had no family, and neither did he."

"Well, Pearly would get the details. You feed her?"

"Pearly?"

"The kid."

"No. She fell asleep after she fell off the counter."

Maudy closed her eyes. "Jesus, Quin. Ain't you got no part of a mind?" The shapely woman walked to the bars of the cell and stood with her arms crossed, watching the sleeping child as the big lawman ate. "She's a mess. Almost the dirtiest child I ever saw."

"I'm going to take her down to the bathhouse and clean her off later."

"God Almighty, a little girl can get diseases sitting in a tub where some pock-ridden cowboy's bathed." Disgusted, Maudy walked to the door. "I got to get back. I'll pick up the tray later. Use that sink in the back to wash her. Don't forget to heat the water. She ain't cast iron. And buy her a dress and some shoes and underwear. Even the orphans' home in San Antone wouldn't take her like she is." She observed Milam's enjoyment of his meal. She added: "And leave something for her to eat."

So Quin left off eating and turned around, looking at Cricket Dawson, thinking about the orphans' home. She was too little for the orphans' home. Where was all the maternal instincts of women, he wondered. Somebody ought to take the kid, want her. Some woman. He, of course, didn't know anything about kids, not girl kids anyway, but women were supposed to know, want kids. When he reached into his pocket for the tobacco pouch and papers to roll a smoke while he thought, he found it again—the letter. Pushing the dinner tray back, he laid the page on the desk. He read it twice.

Sheriff,

Among the winnings from the fatal game at the Bee Hive was a deed to land on the Clear Fork of the Brazos owned by Mr. Dawson. It is quite a large tract. I do not wish to displace Dawson's widow or children. When you have located them and verified their situation and true claim to the land to my satisfaction, I shall return papers restoring their title to a substantial

portion of the property. The rest they may rent or purchase over time at a fair price. Please notify me of the progress of your inquiry.

It was plain to him, as clear as anything he'd ever understood—Mari Marshay wanted to do right by Tim Dawson's widow and kids, wanted him to find out the details for her. She had in effect accepted responsibility for Dawson's widow and children in the letter. Now he had the information she had requested. The child had a guardian even if neither the child nor the guardian knew it.

Milam smoked and thought about the situation of a minor child and a gambling woman owning a ranch in the Brazos country. Could they make it? He sure as hell had not. He looked at the photograph hanging on the front wall of the jail. He didn't know why he'd kept the picture. It didn't show much of a place, just him standing by a rough log structure with a sign proclaiming Running M Ranch over the door with the wavy brand burned in at the end. Behind the house were the two hills that mirrored the shape of the M. *Damn,* he thought.

Delivering the child to its rightful guardian was the justification that Milam had given to his deputies when he had put Vince Martin in charge. Vince was as good as he was at handling things. The community would not suffer in the sheriff's absence. As he had climbed on the stage, Milam had known Vince also wanted his job, but it had not worried him very much for some reason. He would not lose sleep thinking about hanging on to the privilege of wondering what drunk from what alley would shoot him in the back. Delivering the child had been his excuse, but Quin Milam knew in his heart that he had wanted to find the woman again.

Chapter Five

Inside her quarters, Mari sat comfortably in the green leather chair, swiveled it slightly and propped her feet on the green ottoman. Her shoes were pumps, simple, with a comfortable heel, small. She carefully removed the pin from her feathered hat, then the hat. Replacing the pin deftly in it, she set it gently on the plush carpet beside her. Both shapely, well-manicured hands went to her hair, fluffing it, freeing it of the imprint made by the hat.

"I'm Missus Omar Todd," the black clad woman standing in the doorway said. She, too, had removed her hat and coat and looked refreshed from her settling in. "Thought I'd come over and get acquainted. Long train trips can be so lonely. Heaven knows Louisey, my colored girl, has always been silent as a rock. A person needs companions of their own kind. My son's Mister Gilmartin's assistant engineer. He learned so much in the late war that he is absolutely indispensable to the great man even though he's little more than a boy himself. I travel quite a lot since my husband Brigadier General Todd passed on. Omar Todd." She waited expectantly for some acknowledgment from the woman in the chair.

"I'm sorry," Mari Marshay spoke softly. "I

really have not kept up with the military in a long time. Would you care to sit down?"

Mrs. Todd hovered just above the bench seat. "I said to myself you must be well thought of, a respectable woman, to be traveling in the road president's personal car. We ought to get acquainted as respectable women. Your husband must be an important man."

"I'm not married, Missus Todd," answered Mari.

"A widow? So many women lost their husbands in the late war."

"I've never been married. I'm on my own, Missus Todd. I bought a ticket for the trip to Saint Louis. This car was available."

"You have no family?"

"Not really. My mother died shortly after I was born. My father died during the war. I have few relatives that I care to correspond with or who care to correspond with me."

"Family is so important," the woman muttered to herself. "I cannot imagine a life without roots in family and society. You're such an attractive, seemly person. You can't be just a vagabond."

"Vagabond?" Mari repeated the word to herself. "Well, perhaps that is just what I've become . . . a vagabond, drifting about on my own in the world."

Mrs. Todd seemed uncomfortable as her eyes ran over Mari's face. There was a distance in her voice as she spoke. "I really must see what Louisey has done with my dinner dress." Leaving the compartment, she backed into the aisle. The Reverend Beecher saw her coming, but could not avoid her hasty retreat from the woman within. She glared at him imperiously and went to her own cubicle and the silent, comforting company of her maid.

Beecher, in turn, glanced at the woman beyond the open door. His critical eyes met Mari's. She did not resist them.

"Thank you for closing the door," she said softly.

Beecher raked it shut. He continued toward the exit, heading toward the immigrant cars.

The Prairie Queen carried immigrants from the Gulf into the interior of the country. Accommodations in their rough cars were far different from those the special passengers enjoyed. A pot-bellied stove, almost red hot, sat in the center of each swaying coach. A cooking pot, wired to the stovepipe, boiled on it. The smell of cabbage wrinkled Beecher's nose, but he was not weak in the pursuit of his duty. He ventured farther into the dark interior.

There was no fine wood paneling here, only the exposed walls of the car. Two rows of hard wooden benches with strong posts to support the sleeping boxes above were built regularly along the sides. Beecher traversed the center aisle, steadying himself with the posts, as the train rocked gently in its lateral motion clicking over the iron joints. He looked carefully at the families huddled together. Most were long debilitated by the sea voyage and then the overland trip. Their faces showed their deep fatigue as a weary endurance. They were not interested in their surroundings any longer. They only existed—breathing, eating, sleeping away the passing miles until their new lives could begin.

The men wore dirty shirts and rough britches over heavy boots. Their hands were hard and stained around the nail beds and in the deep creases and threaded cracks of the skin. Coal miners, Beecher surmised, coal miners from the old mines of Wales and Middle Europe come to work the new mines at McAlester. Their women were mostly stout, wrapped in layers of garments. Their heads were covered with scarves. The children were gaunt, hungry-looking. Their large eyes searched this stranger in a strange land. Family by family Beecher inquired for English speakers.

"I speak English, preacher," said a man leaning against the rear wall. "What you think of this scum of the Old World come to these pauper jobs to feed the coal to the rich man's steam cars?"

"All men are God's children," Beecher answered. "It's our duty to help the less fortunate."

"I bet you told that to all the damned old Indians on the reservations, too. Made 'em feel much less fortunate. Got to save their heathen souls to boot."

"That's right," Beecher replied. "The red man's world has changed. His only chance now is to change himself, adopt white ways."

"Poor old ignorant-assed Injun," the man said as he straightened. His face came for the first time into the light, into Beecher's vision. Beecher saw that the man was young, a mixed-blood, a 'breed. His hair was long and straight, hanging over his white man's suit coat and collar. "It's a wonder you don't get a nose bleed you're so high above everybody else. Me, preacher, I don't like white men in general and preachers who know so damned much about what everybody else should do, in particular. But like you, I ain't above a real good gawk at the *unfortunates* of this world. Some of their women ain't too bad . . . big tits. Might be a good roll in the hay even . . . in the dark with your eyes shut so you don't see their maggot white skin. Right, preacher?" The 'breed winked.

"You're the man who . . . ," Beecher started his sentence as his mind re-scanned the scene of Watie Boudinot and the whore coupling against the side of a building in full view of the train and its passengers. His mouth closed tightly, and he moved quickly past the man toward the next car.

As the minister closed the door, the 'breed scratched a match into flame and lit the cigar that protruded from a vicious scar at the corner of his mouth. "Now, you big beauties, who's first?"

The few passengers in the presidential car relaxed into the luxury of the first hours of travel, acquainting themselves with their accommodations, watching the changing scenery beyond the open windows. The land was little different from the flat, treeless country in Texas. The heat and rocking motion of the train lulled the travelers into torpor. *Vagabond, vagabond* repeated itself with the voice of the clicking seams of the rails in Mari's ears. *Yes,* the woman thought, *I've become a vagabond. The pilgrim has become a vagabond. But I was always going somewhere. Somewhere. Where?* Her eyes closed, and she dreamed.

Mari rocked gently, listening to the creak of the rigging in the dry air. Above her the orb of the sun glistened like Ahab's golden coin nailed to the mast. Canvas-covered canteens dipped in water hung from the supports of the man-made shade in the hope their contents would be a few degrees cooler than the air around them. They swung with the movement of the ship. It was now the middle of August, and the weather had become insufferably hot, but the replacement unit and its officers were finally out of the Pacific. They had rounded Cape St. Lucas, and sailed up the Gulf of California, toward the mouth of the Colorado, whose red and turbulent waters poured themselves into the bay. From there, the party would take a sternwheeler up river into the interior of Arizona Territory and then, leaving the river, cross the Mojave Desert to their new post at Camp Deserat on the Mogollon Rim. The soldiers called it Camp Desert Rat. Mari's father, an Army surgeon, was especially appointed to the post to study the effects of the desert country on the men stationed there. Accompanying him were his daughter and his assistant surgeon, Phillip Howard. The rest of the party consisted of a few officers, some with their wives.

The heat in the Gulf had been intense, well over a hundred degrees the entire time they waited. The officer's trunks were brought up and summer clothing taken out. But the change proved totally inadequate for the climate. Even under the shade, their faces burned and their scalps blistered down the parts of their hair. The ice supply laid in at San Francisco disappeared quickly. Meat packed in the refrigerator below the quarter-deck turned green and putrid. When the steward opened the door to get provisions for the day, every woman held a bottle of salts to her nose, and the men found business in the forward part of the ship. The ascending odor lingered and would not go away. It followed the passengers to the table, and, when they tasted the food, they tasted the odor of rotting meat.

Thirteen days out of San Francisco, they anchored off Port Isabel at the mouth of the Colorado. Three days of heavy winds churned the sea into angry foam, preventing the passengers from going ashore for the transfer to the flat-bottomed riverboat. The breath of the wind seemed to sweep in over glowing coals. The troopers began to die.

Finally the winds lay. The soldiers and their officers left the steamer for the riverboat. The *Cocopella* steamed upriver towing a barge loaded with the soldiers. Because there were no trees of sufficient size to tie to at night, anchors were taken ashore and made fast. The enlisted men went into camp on shore. It was a low and flat place. That night another man died.

Dr. Claude Marshay's official diary recorded for the 20th of August. **Heat awful—120 degrees at noon. Jerome died today. The lot of the men is a hard one. When they die in this wretched place, they are rolled in a blanket and buried on the desert shores of**

the river with nothing but a heap of stones to mark their graves and protect them from scavenging animals. For many of these men we know little more than a name, a name of their own choosing.

"You must not cry, Mari," Phillip Howard said, putting his arm gently around her waist. "It's a soldier's life. When a man signs up, he knows what can happen."

"Somewhere there must be someone . . . a wife, a mother, a sweetheart . . . someone . . . somewhere who cares. And they will go on caring, not knowing he is dead," Mari whispered.

"Come on now," Howard jostled her slightly. "It's over. Listen, the burial party is returning."

The trumpeters of the command blasted with all their might the strains of "The Girl I Left Behind Me." "Right," said Mari without enthusiasm. "That just makes my point."

"Look." Howard turned her to him. "You know it would not do for soldiers to be sad when one dies. They have to play a tune to cheer themselves up, keep their courage and their course. Tears are out of place at a soldier's funeral."

Mari tipped her forehead against his chest. "You say," she said softly, tears running down her flushed cheeks. "What would their poor lost women say?"

Somewhere two days up the Colorado, when the zinc decks of the vessel burned through the soft soles of the women's shoes, the *Cocopella* greeted and passed barges carrying four companies of infantry returning to the States. Mari stared at the sunburned and unfashionable women with the haggard officers. Their joy was radiant even at a distance. They were going home, wherever that was. Green hills and cool days and nights lay before them as they had left them three years before. The girl wondered if she, too, would look that way when the time for leaving the territory came. She would be a woman then with a husband and perhaps a child of her own.

Chapter Six

"Doctor Howard, sir," the porter said as he opened the physician's door. Howard turned from the small table where he was writing. "Would you get your bag, sir, and come with me. An immigrant woman is having a baby." Howard listened attentively, but made no response. The porter added quickly: "Reverend Beecher sent me for you. He said you would want to come."

"Babies are somewhat out of my line, but I'll get my bag and be down momentarily." Phillip Howard spoke over his shoulder as he returned to his writing.

The steward shifted feet. "Sir," he said, "Mister Beecher said it was urgent."

"And so it is," responded Howard as he finished his task. "Do not worry so much. Women have been having babies for thousands of years." He reached into the small closet for his medical bag. "Bring down some fresh sheets, a couple of basins, and hot water."

As the porter departed on his errand, Howard checked the contents of his kit, and then walked swiftly down the hallway toward the immigrant car. Sliding Mari Marshay's door aside without knocking, he leaned in. She looked up from the book in her lap.

"Come on, Mari. There's a woman having a

baby. I may need your help. She may not speak English."

Without a word, the woman set the book beside her and rose to follow the retreating doctor down the hall, across the moving platform, and through the next cars. Passing through the tiny galley, she opened a compartment and picked up a shallow pan. She shook one of the large teakettles on the stove and spoke to the cook stuffed into a crevice to allow the travelers to pass. "Where are the clean towels?" The man opened a bin, and she took an armload of the white linen. "Bring more boiling water to the immigrant car when it's ready . . . and a pan of ice. Chop it into little pieces." With those words she grabbed one of the teakettles and continued behind Phillip Howard who had gone ahead toward the waiting woman.

The heat and heady smell of human bodies and their belongings in the tightly packed car hit Mari like the weight of a gnarled fist as she opened the door and entered. Her eyes searched the dark interior for Howard and his patient. Beecher appeared from one of the stalls where family groups huddled and motioned for the woman to come forward. Mari stepped over a pair of legs sprawled out across the floor, then over a pair of sleeping children, and around the stove where cabbage simmered. The car itself had become dark with the growing overcast of the day. There were no cheerful cut-glass lamps here as in the presidential car.

"Bring more light," Dr. Howard called out to her as he glanced up from his work.

Mari shifted the teakettle and towels and lifted a kerosene lantern from a hanger. All the way back to the small circle of light around Phillip Howard she stepped over feet and bodies and baggage and managed the rocking motion of the car.

"That's it," Howard affirmed as she lifted the light she carried more for her own sight than his.

Mari Marshay closed her eyes. Before her, legs spread bloody and white, lay a woman not old perhaps, but well past young. Howard had placed sheets around her and over her in an effort to create a clean field for his work. Mari lay the towels carefully on one of the sheets where Howard could reach them. She kneeled quickly, took the instruments from his open bag, and placed them in the shallow pan. Then she poured the boiling water over them. Taking a small bottle from the bag, she poured part of the contents into the water and watched the fluid swirl through the currents of the liquid.

Mari looked up at Beecher whose face had grown ashen. "Why don't you get some air, Mister Beecher? I'm here to help Doctor Howard now. We can call you if you are needed."

"Thank you," whispered the minister, backing away.

When he moved off toward the door, Mari saw the young man slouched casually against a seat. One of his boots was shoved up against a post blocking the seat opposite him. A cigar balancing an inch of ash hung from the corner of his lower lip. His eyes were dark and hooded. The man seemed mildly interested in the scene before him, a spectator at a possibly interesting event like a hog killing.

"Wouldn't you be more comfortable somewhere else?" Mari suggested.

"Not me, sister. I ain't affected by the blood and goo," responded the young 'breed, this different one among the immigrants. "'Fraid I'll see her ass? Shit, I seen plenty of ass."

"Mind your language and move to another seat," Howard told the man flatly, glancing at Mari. The 'breed hesitated. "Do it now." Indolently the man moved one seat forward and shouldered in. He still could throw a glance over the scene, if he twisted a bit. Howard's attention returned to the women. "You haven't gotten squeamish, have you?"

Mari shook her head. "It's been a while, that's all." She rubbed the back of her neck. "I'm fine."

"You won't faint on me?" Howard looked closely at his assistant.

"That'll be the day," responded the woman.

"Good." Howard shoved a basin toward her. "Roll up your sleeves and wash your hands and arms to the elbows." He glanced at the immigrant woman as she moaned. "It's a breech. You'll have to turn it. My hands are too big." Mari looked into his eyes. "No forceps." He spoke in answer to her unasked question. "I'm a soldier's doctor not a woman's. When the chloroform takes hold, I'll do the episiotomy. You can get your hands in then. If that doesn't work, we'll have to do a section."

Howard, like his one-time mentor Dr. Claude Marshay, Mari's father, was a man of science whose personal honor and integrity demanded high standards of professionalism. Early on he had realized the futility of much of his work— the inadequacy of his science's knowledge and methods. He knew, but never accepted, limitations; instead, he worked to push the edges of light into the darkness.

Unlike many of his contemporaries, he did not scoff at new ideas, not even at the mundane thought that simple cleanliness would save lives. He had seen, proved to himself, the value of sanitation. During the war many things had changed. But then every war brought changes in medicine—a kind of repayment for the death and suffering. Early on, in the long wards in Washington, he and a few other doctors had isolated their own patients in certain areas. They had washed their hands before touching each and ordered the nurses to observe the same procedure. Waste and fouled bandages were quickly removed. Hands again washed. Survival rates had climbed whenever basic hygiene was applied. The day was passing when doctors shifted from dissecting disease-ridden cadavers to delivering babies without the ablution of washing hands. If some of their colleagues found the ideas foolish or radical, Phillip Howard did not. He had little use for incompetence or willful ignorance in the face of facts.

"Let me try to turn it before you cut. Maybe I can do it."

"You contradict me as usual," murmured Howard.

"The chances of infection will be less. This isn't exactly a hospital, and you know she won't get care. The less heroic we are the better for her," Mari spoke as she removed a heavy gold bangle from her hand by compressing her fingers. She looked at the bracelet for a few moments, thinking about the size of the circle and her hand before putting it down and finishing the scrub.

"Your father couldn't have said it better," replied Howard.

"Do you have silver nitrate for the eyes?" asked Mari.

"In the bag," responded Howard. "You don't need it now."

"I know," she said softly to herself. When Mari

looked up, the steward stood above her with two kettles of boiling water. She handed him the washbasin. "Dump this and refill it, please, with the hot water. Thank you. Could I also have some of the ice, please."

"So it's going to be please and thank you, eh?" Howard's smile lifted the corner of his mouth as he began to wash the immigrant woman's thighs with the cleansing carbolic water and lye soap Mari had prepared. "Must be serious, Miss Marshay. You're as polite as your father in a crisis."

Taking a fresh towel, Mari carefully dried her hands and walked on her knees to the mother's side. "This is no crisis, Doc. Just a baby mixed up a bit."

"If she hemorrhages, it'll be a crisis," the doctor quipped.

"Could be she won't," Mari said, bending over the woman. "Do you speak English?"

"I kin understand you right enough," the woman whimpered. Her eyes searched Mari's face, but quickly returned to the doctor. "I don't think it proper for him to be putting his hands on me, miss."

Mari took some crushed ice from the pan the steward had left and placed it in the woman's mouth. She folded more ice into the towel and wiped it over the deeply lined face. "He's a good doctor, and he just wants to keep you and your baby from becoming infected with disease. What's your name?"

"Ann. Ann Flanner," came the response.

"Ann," Mari spoke softly, moving the cool wetness of the towel over the woman's face and neck. "You're a bit early." The woman nodded. "So the baby's turned the wrong way." Mari saw the fear dart through the woman's eyes. She continued to apply the cool towel as before. "We are going to have to put it right. We are going to wash you and give you something to put you to sleep so you won't feel any pain. And when you are asleep, I'll turn the baby." Mari's eyes met and held the woman's eyes. "It's not pleasant, but it will work, Ann. I'll see to it."

Ann Flanner nodded. "Dear God in heaven. Do what ye must. I don't want a dead one inside me ever again. It were the evil eye what caused this. My man's old mother told me. And I knowed it, too. I should have been more careful." The woman's eyes ran over Mari's face, looking for some confirmation of the cause and her guilt.

"Ann, no evil eye caused this. The baby decided to come before it got in position . . . maybe the traveling hurried it, or maybe it just happened as it does sometimes." Mari stroked the words into the woman with her soft voice and the cool towel. Howard handed Mari the small screen mask and cotton to place over the woman's nose and mouth. Mari held it a moment in her lap. "Do you want a boy or a girl when you wake up?"

"I want no more of either," the woman said honestly. "Are ye a married woman?"

"No." Mari shook her head.

The woman's eyes wandered into the darkness as she sighed. "Can't understand it then, I reckon. I get pregnant every two or three months, and then in a few weeks, lose it. Still I got five children, besides this one, in eight years. My man will have it, and the priest will have it, but it will kill me same as it killed my own mother and all her kind." She rested, focused on the darkness as Mari laid the towel on her forehead and gently pressed her hand over it. "Soon I'll be gone, and who'll take care of my little children, miss? Who? Not a home to go to . . . or food laid up . . . nor cash money, neither. What man can handle six children without a woman?"

"Well, Ann, you will not die tonight . . . nor your child, either. And when this is over, the doctor will talk to you. Right, Doc?" Mari's eyes burned the question into Phillip Howard's face.

"My man will not stand for it," the woman whispered confidentially to Mari. "It will only cause fussin'."

"That's a worry for another day. But you've decisions to make." Mari looked up as Howard coughed to draw her attention. "Not only for yourself and your husband, but for those six children."

"Leave your social work for another time, Miss Marshay."

"Now, Ann, the doctor says we must get to work," Mari said.

"I never had no doctor before. They say that them what has the doctors is them that dies the firstest," whispered Ann Flanner.

"Not this doctor." Mari slipped the mask over the woman's nose.

"All right," Howard spoke gruffly. "Here's the chloroform. You remember enough to keep your own nose out of it?"

Mari nodded absently as she began the drip. They sat quietly waiting for the woman to lose consciousness. There was no timeline, just a waiting and a watching for signs the anesthesia was taking effect. Howard wiped his patient's face with the iced towel then lifted her arm. It fell back limply to the car floor. Mari shifted toward the woman's legs and sluiced her own hands and arms again in the washbasin. Howard lifted the covering sheet and the lamp. Gently Mari moved her hands over the distended abdomen, palpating the baby.

"You can't get to it," Howard said. "I'll make the incision."

Mari ignored him. Compressing the fingers and thumb of her right hand, she pushed gently into the birth canal. With her left, she continued contact with the abdomen. "If the cervix is dilated as much as that bracelet, I can get my hand inside."

"Be careful of the cord. Don't cut off the baby's air," instructed Howard as he watched her movements. Mari remained silent, ignoring him. "Well?"

"I can do it," Mari said quietly. She smiled. "We're going to have a baby, Doc." Howard sat back on his heels with a small sigh. "I still need the light, Doc."

Howard leaned forward, watching the light play over Mari's clear face. Sweat ran down her hairline and stood above her upper lip. Her white blouse was wet through with perspiration in the intense heat of the car and the work. Its sheerness disclosed a lace camisole. He permitted himself a long look at the form of Mari Marshay. Her arms were strong and shapely, her body lean and supple. She was more beautiful than he remembered. But the beauty was not so much in her features. Mari was glazed, coated, animated in some way by that fearful life intensity that had grown stronger with the years. He turned away. The minutes stretched out.

"There," proclaimed Mari, disclosing the glistening red baby. Howard tied a sterile string from the iodine-saturated water of the basin around the umbilical cord as Mari lifted and held the child. He quickly cut the cord and dipped the stump in fresh iodine. Mari worked over the baby's nose and mouth, pulling away the membrane, then removing the mucus from the openings. The baby remained lifeless.

"Slap it, Mari," instructed Howard, reaching for the child.

Instead, Mari turned from him and reached into the ice basin and flicked some of the chilled water on to the child. It twisted in her hand. "Say something, baby," she whispered. The little mouth opened on command, and a hearty howl came forth. Smiling, Mari looked up into Howard's intense gaze.

"Where'd you pick that up?" he asked.

"Apaches use water, cool spring water, if they can get it, to wake the sleeper," she said, and watched his eyes cloud again with protective indifference.

"Well done, then," Howard said abruptly, taking the baby from her hands. "Should I ever deliver another baby, I'll try to remember that pagan ritual. I think I can handle it from here, Miss Marshay. Thank you very much." Howard turned to the newborn as Mari washed the blood from her hands and arms, and then rolled down her sleeves. Her lips were slightly set as she rose and walked away from the doctor and his patients. As he bent over the immigrant woman, Howard heard the door close softly.

Chapter Seven

Leaning against the rail of the rocking railway car platform, Mari studied the landscape without seeing it—the dismissal by Phillip Howard had irritated her more than she wished to admit. She also bore a pervasive feeling of sadness, of something missed—some hope, some opportunity. She could never quite place her problems with Phillip in words. There had always been vague feelings of guilt, discontent, or irritation, and even now they were the same, familiar companions of their relationship.

Phillip was skillful. She respected him greatly as a doctor. During the delivery, he had counted upon her, even accepted her thoughts. But there was no mutuality. She was never satisfied that he valued her abilities. She always felt like a dog that had performed a trick of minimal difficulty for a superior being.

Mari was not a woman who needed compliments or reassurance. She was an independent woman who pretty well did as she pleased. Her father had not raised her to expect compliments or even the words well done. In his reasoning, a job well done was simply the correct way to do it. If it were not correct, he would put her straight. After all, in life one was not applauded for doing things right. That was expected. It was a matter of personal honor and character to do what was right in any circumstance. There was no need for more. But with her father it had always been enough that she knew she had done her task well. She wondered why she needed some kind of recognition from Howard.

And there was the other issue with Phillip, the sense of betrayal he conveyed at unexpected turns. She had not betrayed him. She knew that. Why, then, did she still feel the guilt? It was contagious with the man. Mari sighed and drummed her knuckles gently against the rail.

"Ah, dear lady, do you not like my country?" The soft voice of Boudinot asked.

"Yes, very much," Mari answered, turning from her reverie to face the large man.

Boudinot's presence filled the rocking platform. It was warm and fragrant like open fields and skies with a touch of tobacco and cherry water after-shave. He extended his hand. "For want of a better introduction, I am Eli Boudinot. At your service, ma'am." He bowed slightly without taking his eyes from her face. "I cannot help thinking we have met before, during the war perhaps."

"Mari Marshay." The woman shook his hand. His grip was firm, powerful in purpose as well as strength. He did not hold her a breath too long, but released her hand quickly, softly. "Afraid not. I was in the West during the war."

Boudinot gently turned her toward the rail and the land beyond. "I began there at Pea Ridge, then moved on. But that is past, over, mercifully forgotten. Is it not beautiful, this land?" Boudinot was all around her. There was no hint of overstepping or of the predatory nature the woman had long ago learned to sense and avoid. She turned to look into his face, but his eyes were on the land. "God, I love it! Every rock, every tree, every rolling hill, every sparkling stream falling over the flint rocks, rising in steam in the morning hollows." He looked down at her, embarrassed by his own enthusiasm. "You are bad for me. I generally don't run on like this. But I'm going home. I freely admit to you, a comparative stranger on a train that I am child-like, unburdened by the prospect of my return, of being on home ground. It is so beautiful there. You should see it."

"Perhaps I shall," Mari agreed. "It is beautiful from here."

"Oh, but it is more beautiful there . . . in the green hill country. It is a hidden treasure." He smiled at her. The train swerved slightly, throwing Mari back against the rail. Boudinot's great arm encircled her waist and drew her back to a safer position. For a brief moment, they stood very close with Mari's hand upon his forearm. "You must be more careful, Miss Marshay. Now I must go forward to attend to something. I hope to see you at dinner." Eli Boudinot stepped easily to the other platform and reached for the door handle, but turned back. "Do hold on more securely, please. There is real danger."

After Boudinot disappeared, the woman's hands came to her face, resting on her eyes for several moments, at last wiping away the discomforting thoughts of Howard. She cocked her head slightly as she gazed at the land. Had she met Eli Boudinot before? She did not think so. She gripped the rail a little tighter as the car swayed.

"Hey, lady," the words of Jimmy Wing broke into Mari's thoughts. "Buy a book, a paper, some fruit to tide you over till dinner."

Mari turned to view the tray that hung from the boy's shoulders. "So what do you have?" she asked, studying the assortment of merchandise Jimmy hawked to the passengers.

"Oranges," the boy offered. "Sweet as sugar."

"One orange, then," Mari said, beginning to peel the fruit as she looked over the other contents of the tray. "Any new books?"

"Dime novels mostly." Jimmy turned through the small set of volumes as she bit into a section of orange. "Say, when I looked into the immigrant car, I could see you were having some trouble with that 'breed."

"He was not a very pleasant person." Mari opened the cover of a small volume with her little finger, protecting it from the sticky orange juice. "My Lord, you have *The Woman in White* by Wilkie Collins."

"Yeah, kind of scary stuff. If I was a woman, I'd sure be careful who I married in England. Did you get the 'breed's name?"

"No." Mari looked up. "Why are you so interested in that man?"

"Just curious." Jimmy shrugged. "He seems out of place to me."

Mari continued to browse the books. "Well, it is a train. Nobody really has a place on a train except the crew, now, do they? We are all just passengers going somewhere from somewhere. A metaphor for life, I guess. What's your name?"

"Jimmy Wing. Do you think he resembles Boudinot?"

Mari frowned and thought a moment. "Well, I was pretty busy, so I didn't look closely at him. I guess they are both dark. Maybe his eyes were blue like Mister Boudinot's."

"Oh, they are blue, all right. That's the first thing you notice . . . how blue their eyes are for Injuns."

"You think the two men are related?"

"Maybe."

"There's a world of difference in their attitudes and behavior."

"Yeah, well, Eli Boudinot's a tested man. The other one ain't."

Mari smiled. "What's a tested man?"

"Boudinot was in the war, a hero left for dead."

"And how do you know so much about Eli Boudinot?"

"I saw him once on his way to court in Fort Smith. And I have ears. I hear things."

"You've heard a lot of things about Mister Boudinot," observed Mari as she finished the orange and tossed the peel over the railing.

"Yeah." Jimmy Wing sat back on the rail. "And about you, too."

"Me? What could a young boy hear about me that would be worthwhile?" Mari leaned on the opposite railing, looking at the country beyond.

"You're a rich gambler."

"No!" Mari said in disbelief. "Me . . . a gambler?" Her smile faded. "I'm not a gambler any more, unless you call riding a train that can run off a shoddy track or bridge, telescope one car into another, or catch fire, burning all passengers to death, when a stove breaks apart in a collision, gambling."

"You're a doctor, then," postulated the youth.

"My father was a doctor. I sometimes helped him when I was growing up," responded Mari.

"I can't see my little sisters doing that or anyone letting a young girl witness such things," whispered the boy.

"You're a prude, Jimmy Wing. But I'm not

sure that my father ever thought of me as a young girl . . . more of an available set of hands and feet. Anyhow, I seemed to take to it," replied Mari, looking into the passing countryside. "Well, Jimmy Wing, here's your money. Thanks for the orange and the book." The woman opened the door and disappeared into the interior of *The Prairie Queen*.

Entering the passenger carriage, Mari caught a glimpse of the partially opened door of a compartment. A dark eye peered shyly out. Mari observed quietly. "Hello," she said to the eye. The door closed quickly.

Just as she moved down the aisle, a man's deep voice spoke gently through the closed door. "Child, that is no way to act. Open the door now and talk to the lady, if you wish to know her. You must learn to be forward in the white man's world. Look them in the eyes. You must always look white people in the eye. They consider it a sign of good character, not bad manners."

Mari leaned back against the paneling, listening to the gently given advice, waiting for its results. Slowly the glass began to move back. Mari stood silently. Slowly the form of an Indian girl of thirteen or fourteen was revealed. She was very straight and stunningly beautiful. Mari smiled. The girl, too, smiled and started to lower her eyes, but quickly brought them back to Mari's face.

"My mother is a healer," she said. "She sometimes delivers babies, too. The porter said you sprinkled the baby with cold water to make it cry. I have seen her do that."

"I was taught that by an Apache woman," answered Mari. "It is a good way to wake the sleeper even for white people."

"Yes," the girl agreed, and started to close the door.

"Show hospitality, daughter, invite the woman into your compartment," the deep voice offered.

"Please, miss." The girl turned, revealing the inner room and gesturing slightly to it. "I am Susan Marn, and this is my father, Joshua Stanley Marn. We would be pleased to have you sit with us in our compartment."

Mari entered and sat where the child indicated. The old mountain man was stretched out on the bench seat. He shifted himself into a sitting position, and the girl sat beside him. "Offer the lady something to drink, Susan."

Mari shook her head slightly. "No thank you. Dinner won't be long now. Are you ill, Mister Marn?"

"Hell, no," replied the ancient mountain man. "Blind as a bat. Can't see you, but you smell nice. What's your name, lady?"

Mari smiled. "My name is Mari . . . Mari Marshay."

"Well, as the child has told you, I'm Marn," the

man said. "Most folks call me that . . . or Josh that know me."

The woman relaxed in the leather chair. "Josh Marn? I've heard that name."

"Not in a long time you ain't," the old one attested. "I ain't been worth much in twenty damn' years. If it weren't for the Injuns, I'd been dead long time ago. But they've took to me and me to them."

Mari studied the man's deeply tanned and lined face. His white beard covered much of the lower contours, but did not hide the strong nose and patrician forehead. His eyes were opaque with thick cataracts. "You were on one of the first Western expeditions, never came back, but became a trapper, a mountain man," she remembered. "You have a trading house, quite a famous place as I recall . . . Marn's Fort."

"You know a lot for an Easterner," observed the old man.

"What makes you think I'm an Easterner?" the woman asked.

"Well, you smell too good to get too far from civilization."

"A Western woman can buy perfume the same as anyone else." Mari smiled.

"They can, but they don't generally, unless they work in saloons, and then it has a cheap, bawdy smell. You smell like flowers on the night wind. That'd be a good Injun name. Susan's Indian name means Many Clouds in a Tall Sky Moving Slowly Over the Prairies. That's too much to say for a white man, ain't it? I call her Susan, or more likely just Daughter, but she's got a pretty name, anyhow."

"Daughter is a good name if you think about it," Mari commented, "implying many good things . . . affection, devotion, identity. And it looks as if she is doing very well in her rôle." The girl ducked her head at the compliment.

"Oh, them Injuns think I'm somethin' on a stick. They dote on this old carcass of mine. My wives are more than good to me and have taught the child." He stopped, then added: "It's offensive to some folks that I've more than one wife, but I do."

"I'm not offended," Mari stated.

The old man paused, considering her words. "Well, that's a wonder for a white woman."

Mari smiled. "Yes, we can be hard on a man. Something to do with our raising, I suppose."

"That's a fact." Marn nodded. "But white raisin' ain't all bad. Right now and who knows for how long, the white people hold the whip hand, and they ain't likely to give it up. Being white, I know how tenacious we are as a race. A child must be prepared for the world and not just the world we'd like it to be. It's good to give them aspirations and ideals, but it is also good to give them a good grounding in survival. I'm

93

taking Susan back to Saint Louis to school, the nuns, to complete her education. She's to have a good one, same as her brothers. A man owes it to his children to prepare them for the stony road ahead. I would not send them out without knowledge and supplies in the mountains, and I will not send them out into the white man's world unprepared and unknowing of its ways. Be like putting them out to die."

Mari considered the man's words and noted that the "ain't" and the accent of the frontier trader were smoothing out into a refined pattern of speech. "You have great wisdom, Mister Marn."

"I believe we are going to be friends, so you had better call me Josh. Daughter, I'd like a glass of water. My throat is dry. See that the lady has something to drink." The child filled a glass for her father, then looked up into Mari's blue eyes and smiled. The smile ornamented Susan's face, lighting it from within. "Ask her if she wants something stronger?"

The girl set the pitcher back on the table. "Father wonders if you would you care for something else, Miss Marshay?"

"Thank you, water will be fine for me, also," returned Mari. The girl poured the water carefully, gracefully.

"My children all have good manners and speak good English," Marn said. "I know it is not expected of mixed-bloods . . . most being the fruit of transient couplings . . . but I'm a man to claim what is mine for good or bad. Can't say as there has been a bad. The children are all exceptional, my three sons and my daughter. In the beginning I made a bargain with myself that I would respect the People and their ways and deal with them like I would with any good man. It is a bargain I have not gone back on. I do not pile stones on their chests by feeling sorry for them or treating them as children of the forest . . . what claptrap . . . nor as inferiors for many have taught me better ways than I knew. I have found them to be as other men, some good, some bad, some honorable, some scoundrels, most just barely squeaking by with little or no idea of what is going on. My children have my name. The boys named after my father and me and my brother. My daughter named for my mother. They will take my place in life. I expect them to go beyond what I have done, but I do not expect them to make the journey without my best guidance and support. I'm a simple man."

"Those are the words of a thoughtful man who has refined simplicity from complexity, but they are not the words of an untutored mountain man. That, sir, I think, is your pose, your disguise."

"Your young eyes see through an old man and his thoughts. But I have been so long in the West that whatever education I had has slowly seeped away with the rain and the snow or blown away with the dust and wind. The West will do that to a man . . . strip him bare of his favorite pretensions. . . ."

"Perhaps the West strips away only the superfluous affectations of civilization. Maybe it just clarifies us."

"Have you been in the West much?"

"My father was an Army doctor. We were at a desert outpost for some time. We traveled some. It was a hard and uncompromising country . . . no place for a woman, they say. But I believe the land and the life have a grandeur that comfortable people will never know. Is that what kept you in the West?"

"Maybe. The people and the places, even the ideas, just seemed so small when I went back to my old country. It was like I'd grown two sizes and couldn't fit myself back into my old clothes. Everything was tight and tugging at me. I needed to breathe."

"Josh," Mari began, and then paused. "There are things civilization can do. Perhaps you could see a doctor for your eyes in Saint Louis."

"I reckon I have worn calluses on them from seeing so much. Once I killed an old bear . . . his eyes were all callused over like mine are now. When I skinned him out, it looked to me like the calluses would peel right off. I'm hopin' there is someone in Saint Louis who can peel away my blindness. I'd like to see the distances again, see my wives' and children's faces. But if not, I have seen this country in all its glory and greatness . . . long before white men moved in with their bawling beasts and plows. What I have seen is vivid in the eyes of my mind. It can never be dimmed or ruined there."

Mari was thoughtful. "There are some doctors who are beginning to do procedures to remove cataracts. Perhaps you will find one in Saint Louis, or someone there will know where to send you. Many things are happening in Philadelphia."

"Do you live in Saint Louis?"

"I have some property there." Mari rose as she spoke the words. "Please excuse me now. I must dress for dinner, and I have not had time to see to my clothes."

"Miss . . . ?" Josh began.

"Mari," interrupted the woman.

"Yes, Mari, would you take the child to dinner? I'm so blind, I do not eat at table with company. I will have a tray here. But I think Susan should sit down to dinner on the train. I've been wondering how to accomplish that without embarrassing her and myself with my fumbling."

Mari looked at Susan. "Would you like that?"

"Oh, yes, Miss Marshay. I have a new dress."

"Very well. I shall pick you up when the porter announces dinner." Mari closed the door behind her and walked quickly to her own room.

Chapter Eight

Returning from the birthing, Phillip Howard crossed through the passenger carriage. He felt an odd sense of guilt as he passed Mrs. Todd's open door. She scrutinized him critically. He shrugged it off. The door to the quarters shared by Boudinot and Joe Crites stood convivially open. Crites stripped to undershirt and galluses was lathering his face for a shave before dinner. Already dressed, Boudinot smoked while thumbing through a newspaper. The doctor only nodded as he went by.

"Boy or girl, Doc?" called out Crites. "I put money on it being a boy."

Howard stopped with his hand on the doorknob of the rear platform door. He thought a long moment before looking back at Crites. "Sorry," he said softly. "I don't seem to be able to remember whether it was a boy or a girl. Boy, I think. Well, it's one or the other, isn't it? Mister Beecher can probably tell you when he returns."

He passed Mari's closed door without a glance at the shaded windows. After entering his small private room and closing the door and shades, Phillip Howard sprawled onto the daybed and stared at the ceiling.

The sun darted bright spears of light off the shallow water of the creek. Phillip Howard squinted and turned his eyes back to Mari. She filled his senses even in the heat of the baked land beyond the stream. They were not talking, had not talked for a long time as they walked. He let her go a few steps ahead just to watch her move, to take in her beauty. Walking with her head down, looking at the broken twigs and rocks at her feet, she seemed thoughtful.

"Having regrets?" asked the young officer.

She stopped and turned back toward him, cocking her head slightly. "Regrets?"

He closed the distance between them. "Marriage is a big step. Are you sure you are ready? It's just two weeks . . . your eighteenth birthday, the wedding, and then a lifetime. You're so young, Mari, a lifetime can be intimidating."

She smiled. "I love you, Phillip. I could only regret not loving you, not marrying you, not having a lifetime with you."

Phillip Howard drew her to him. He held her for a long moment, looking into her face, then bent gently and kissed her lips. He felt her warmth returned to him. He kissed her with more eagerness, and again he felt her own eagerness. Howard's hand moved up her waist and caressed her body gently, delicately, then more passionately. She did not pull away. His mouth moved down her neck into the opening of her blouse, lips brushing the smooth skin. He drew back the cloth and moved onto the bareness. She stiffened slightly, ever so slightly. The movement was hardly detectable. Then she pulled away from him.

"Bourke says a man will test a maid. Is this my test?" she asked gently.

Howard felt caught out, irritated. "Damn Bourke! He's your father's striker . . . not your mother or my conscience. What does two weeks matter, Mari? In two weeks we'll be married. I want you now, this minute, this place," Phillip persuaded softly. "Must you pull away and torment me? What does two weeks and a ceremony mean at this point?"

The girl pulled her blouse together. She concentrated over the buttons as Howard reasoned with her out of his own need. When she lifted her head, she was smiling. "Now, Doc, two minutes would mean a lot to you. That's the kind of man you are. You'd always wonder whether you were persuasive, or I was just a slut."

"God in heaven, Mari, such language." Her words on top of the accusation hit Howard like cold water. He was irritated, angry, then in charge again. "You are going to have to watch that."

"See, Doc. Two minutes ago you were ready

to devour me, and now you wonder what people will think about the way I talk." She walked farther down the creek with Howard trailing.

"Dammit, Mari. You're going to be my wife in two weeks. This squeamishness is false. You have desires just like I have." She did not answer him, but stopped to listen. Howard smiled temptingly. "Maybe we can go riding again tomorrow."

"No," the girl said flatly, and began to walk again. "It's getting too hard to say no to you."

Dr. Howard muttered and untied her horse, handing her the reins. "You must have ice water in your veins."

Mari held his hand, then kissed it lightly. "If you think that, you've lost your touch, Doc." Before he could speak, she caught his shoulder, stepped onto the boulder beside the horse, and seated herself in the side-saddle. "Last one back walks Colonel Elliot's bulldog."

With these words she was away, and Phillip Howard was clamoring onto his horse for the race.

Phillip Howard opened his eyes. The stifling heat of the small compartment had overcome him with a restless sleep. A full and oppressive fatigue coated him like the sweat that seeped from his

101

pores. *So it starts again. I haven't the energy for this.* He sat up and put his feet on the floor, resting his elbows on his knees. *Why this train? What are the chances of running into the wrong woman twice in your life, Howard?*

Buck up, old boy, the perverse nature in him said. *She says she doesn't love you, and you know Mari can be too honest.*

"Shut up," Howard said aloud to the empty room, and sloshed water from the basin onto his face.

Louisey opened the door to Mari Marshay's compartment. "Iron you dress for dinner for a quaader?" she called out.

Mari removed her glasses and rubbed her eyes. "I guess it's too much to expect a knock."

Louisey grinned and knocked on the door she leaned against. "Well, sugar, you want you dress ironed?"

"Sure." Mari stretched. "I hung it in the closet so it would drop out some of the wrinkles."

Humming, Louisey came into the room and opened the tiny closet to get the deep green dress. "Uhm. This is a fine dress. Looka here, the way them seams is done, just perfect. Who make you dress?"

"A seamstress in San Antonio."

"She black?"

"No."

"I didn't think so. Them black gals can't sew worth nothing."

"Why not? Are they incapable of using the skills common to other women and even to some men?" Louisey turned and looked at Mari who sat watching her. "What would you have said if I'd said a black woman did make it?"

"I'd've said them black gals can sure sew fine."

Mari smiled. "You are a great liar, Louise. You just tell us *pore ole* white folks what we want to hear, don't you?"

"You too fast for me, missy." Louisey looked down at the dress she was holding.

"Look at me, Louise," Mari said softly. "Don't pull that nigger routine with me. You are smart enough for six white people. I can see I'm going to have to hustle to keep up with you."

Louise wanted to change the conversation from herself. "I heard them stewards talkin' 'bout you. They say you is rich. That's what they say. They say you ain't got no man. You is a independent woman."

Mari considered the other woman's words. "Yes, I suppose I am an independent woman."

"That's a good thing to be. Ain't askin' can I do this or that. Ain't worried about somebody goin' to feed you or give you some place to live. Hum-hum. Ain't just free, but independent . . . not needing nothing or no one. Ain't that right?"

"I'll have to think about that," Mari answered.

103

"I suppose it is the nature of life that we need each other. We all owe and are owed."

"Like helpin' that poor woman and her baby," postulated Louise. "She owe you."

"I don't consider that a debt," said Mari. "That was just a decency to someone in need, maybe just a small repayment to the house on a debt."

"You a rich woman in debt?"

"Of course, I'm a great debtor, Louise. I can never repay the house. The debt grows every day, so maybe I'm not so independent, after all."

"You is a nice woman anyways," surmised Louise.

"What makes you think I'm nice for heaven's sake? Your mistress couldn't sit down in the same room with me."

"Anyone can see that by the way you carries youself like you respec' who you is. And you clothes is cut to fit, but you ain't strainin' every seams. You've got taste . . . nothin' ain't obvious, but everything just so. Some gals is busting out of their satin and spilling over into folkes' faces. And you ain't been too good to help that poor old woman and her baby. You even talk to me like I was a human bein', not a nigger. Only a lady do that. You is sure enough of youself not to be afraid other folkes is goin' to rub off." Louise departed with the dress to do her work.

Mari stripped down to her underwear and donned a silk robe for her trip to the train's nearest bath. She passed the closed door of the final compartment with some curiosity since she had heard no sound nor seen any occupant since the journey began. The porter who sat at the end of the car in order to respond immediately to his passengers' needs came quickly forward.

"Can I help you, miss?" he asked.

"Oh, no," Mari answered, "I was just wondering if something might be wrong with the traveler in that compartment. I've yet to see him, and it's amazingly hot . . . stifling . . . in this area."

"The passenger doesn't wish to be disturbed, ma'am. Just wants the door and windows kept tight shut. No drafts. No visitors."

"Yes, well, thank you," said Mari. "I didn't mean to interfere . . . just curious, I guess."

The porter nodded, and Mari went along the corridor to the bath.

John Beecher returned heavily burdened from his mission in the immigrant cars. He came into the space shared by Crites and Boudinot. "I don't understand that woman."

Crites turned from the tiny mirror, soap still covering one side of his round face. "What's the matter, Mister Beecher?"

"I imagine he objects to The Pagan's morals," Boudinot said without looking up from the paper he was reading.

"Well . . ." Crites held his razor thoughtfully.

105

"You've got to admit that she is good-looking. Real classy dame, The Pagan. I'm a married man and can't be sure, but I swear I saw her at Fort Griffin. She was playing poker, and the game went sour. Two of the men drew guns. Everybody was on the floor like lightning, when they heard the chairs scoot back and the crack of the pistols. Everybody but The Pagan. Those card-playing gentlemen shot each other dead on the spot. The Pagan sat calmly through it all. Replaced her cards on the table . . . face up . . . and when it was over claimed the pot. What a woman!" Joe Crites concluded as he drew the razor down his cheek.

"The Pagan!" Beecher wheezed. "That is exactly it! How on God's earth can The Pagan do what you've just described and a short while later appear the good and beneficent woman I saw in the immigrant car? She is opaque to me, yet I know extremely dangerous. Howard should know." Beecher left the compartment.

"Guess a man like that can be trouble for a certain kind of woman," Crites said quietly.

Boudinot's dark eyes looked up over the paper. He considered Crites's words without comment. One eyebrow cocked slightly before he returned to reading.

"Hey, Beecher!" Joe Crites leaned out the door and called to the minister. "Was it a boy or a girl?"

"Girl," replied the departing clergyman without a glance backward.

Crites smiled and extended his palm toward Boudinot. The Indian placed a coin in his hand. "You are a fine gentleman, sir," chuckled Crites.

Boudinot, too, smiled. "We'll see, Mister Crites."

Beecher's mind was on a thank you to Howard and a warning when he opened the platform door and entered the presidential car. Just as he entered, Mari emerged from the tiny lavatory. Beecher stopped abruptly and drew himself up, startled by her shocking state of undress even though she was fully covered by the dressing gown tied loosely over her undergarments. He lowered his eyes quickly, avoiding looking at her, then hastily moved along the aisle toward the lounge. Mari barely noticed Beecher as she again felt the same overpowering heat emanating from the unknown passenger's room. *Surely there's no stove in there,* she said to herself, wiping the sweat that had appeared on her face.

"You throw water on him?" asked Louise innocently, standing inside Mari's compartment with the green dress.

"Who?"

"That preacher," responded Louise, helping Mari into the dress.

"Must be something he ate," Mari answered

absently, still thinking about the closed room.

"Or something eating him." The black woman bent to flip a fold in the dress as she considered the thought.

Mari smoothed the fitted bodice of her dress. "I'm sure Mister Beecher is a sincere man."

"Well, honey, you've got half of it right. Beecher's a man."

Dr. Howard stood smoking thoughtfully, leaning against his door as Beecher approached.

"I wanted to thank you for helping the woman have her baby. You more than likely saved her life and the child's." Beecher hesitated a moment, then plunged on with his thoughts. "Are you aware of the history of the woman who assisted you? I have it on authority that she is the infamous Pagan. Shameful!" sputtered the clergyman.

Howard drew a deep draft on the cigar. "Miss Marshay? Really, sir?"

"Certainly. Her past is as black as the night beyond that window," Beecher responded.

"Actually I was assisting *her*. By the way, we haven't formally met." Howard extended his hand. "Doctor Phillip Howard."

The preacher grasped the offered hand. "Beecher. Reverend John Beecher."

As the gesture concluded, Howard smiled. "Ah, that explains your vast understanding. You are the trained observer of guilt and shame of the human soul. I, on the other hand, am a mere observer of the human animal."

"I realize that in your profession you must be a scoffer, a mocker, Doctor. But God is not mocked. And man is not a mere animal. He is a created being with an immortal soul. Perhaps you should be on guard against what such a woman can do to a man's soul."

"The right woman, I've heard it said, can save a man's soul."

"That is not the right woman. Her soul has no light to shed . . . no hope to offer, sir," the minister stated flatly. "She's a merciless gambler."

A flicker of interest flashed in Howard's next words. "You know, Reverend Beecher, in the many times I have cut into bodies, I have never seen a soul. I wonder how you can locate and diagnose it, or its absence, so precisely. Does it vary . . . small and shriveled in the ungodly . . . plump and juicy in the righteous?"

"Make light of me . . . of what you don't understand through your training, Doctor. I read funeral services not a week ago in San Antonio over a man that was broken by that woman they call The Pagan. She destroyed him. Perhaps he was also a scoffer."

"Really?" queried Howard casually. "The Pagan?"

"Yes, sir. The Pagan. The one who helped you

deliver the baby . . . *that* is The Pagan. She and the kind of danger a woman like that carries are on this train in this very car. You toy with me to your own ruin," Beecher stated with satisfaction.

Howard straightened, dusted his jacket front of a stray cigar ash. "You must be mistaken. I know that woman. I served in her father's regiment. A gentleman, he raised her to be a lady."

A porter paused in the aisle the men blocked. "Dinner is ready in the dining car at your convenience, gentlemen."

"Must change my jacket," muttered Beecher as he padded behind the porter down the aisle. Howard continued to enjoy his aromatic cigar. Slowly he put out the cigar and straightened his own jacket before following.

"Let's put on the feedbag, boys." Joe Crites rubbed his hands together in anticipation of the feast in the dining car as the porter and Beecher passed. Crites and Eli Boudinot started forward.

Chapter Nine

Mari stopped at the compartment of Joshua Marn, and tapped lightly on the door. It slid back, revealing the old mountain man and his daughter. "Well, lady, is she not beautiful?" asked the old man. "A jewel among women."

Mari considered the girl. "Oh, my, yes. Your daughter is exquisite, Josh."

"What about the dress? Is it fashionable enough for a fine dinner?"

"Its simplicity makes it fashionable anywhere," answered Mari. She turned the girl about with the tips of her fingers. "What good taste you have, Susan Marn."

The girl blushed. "It was the prettiest picture of a dress I ever saw," she confessed. "Papa got the material for us, and my mother and I made it."

"Wow!" a voice exclaimed from the corridor.

Mari turned to see young Jimmy Wing. The boy stood transfixed by the girl and her beauty. "Wow," he repeated. On this occasion he wore the immaculate white coat of a steward.

"You've changed jobs, Mister Wing," Mari noted.

"One of the regular guys got sick. Puking his guts up." The boy's eyes had not left Susan Marn.

"Graphic, Mister Wing." Mari sighed. "Nonetheless, you are just the man we need to see.

Mister Marn will want his supper served here. Will you attend to that? Susan will go in to dinner with me."

Mari and Susan Marn entered the dining car just behind Phillip Howard who had stopped in the doorway. He turned to watch them. Seeing the beautiful mixed-blood child of Josh Marn, his eyes darted quickly to Mari's. There was a question deep within them. She saw it, understood it, before he spoke.

"Your daughter, Mari?"

She cocked her head slightly and smiled. "What do you think, Doc? Same eyes?"

Howard looked down at the floor. "I don't know what to think."

"I think you'll miss your dinner, but we won't." Mari led the girl past the Army surgeon toward two empty chairs. They sat at the elegantly appointed table across from Joe Crites and the small, French priest, Father Reyneau.

"Can you understand that bird?" inquired Crites, setting the saltshaker closer to Mari.

"Perhaps." Mari turned to the priest. "*Bon soir, m'sieu*. Are you enjoying your travels?" she continued in French.

"*Ah, mademoiselle, c'est bon*, such a large country!" The little man bubbled over at this one among the heathens with whom he could speak.

Mari listened and responded politely as the Frenchman continued his soliloquy on the

112

arduous travel, the strange country and customs.

"And how is it you speak French with such ease?" asked Father Reyneau.

"I lived in New Orleans as a child. Later I accompanied my father to Europe," Mari responded.

"Yes, I have just come through New Orleans. Saint Louis Cathedral is amazingly handsome. The city is a beautiful city . . . European in many ways."

"Beautiful, but deadly," observed Mari. "The fever takes a melancholy harvest there. The doctors have no successful treatment. Wise people still flee New Orleans during the summer."

"I should have liked to have stayed and helped the people. But I am going to Saint Louis. My sister lives there. I have not seen her for almost thirty years . . . since she was a child, since I entered the priesthood, since Rome." The priest's thoughts wandered away from the conversation for a long moment. "She has grown children. The years go so quickly."

"Yes," Mari said thoughtfully. "Years pass unnoticed."

Phillip Howard found a seat between Beecher and Mrs. Todd. Occasionally he glanced at Mari Marshay. Conversing with his companions, he studied Susan Marn. The eyes, the eyes. He could see nothing. He struggled silently with Mari, wanting her to show some sign of the dissolute life she had taken up, of the years alone without him. But the woman defied him. Every gesture was gracious and revealed her breeding and training. She spoke pleasantly with the priest, at ease in the situation, putting him at ease as any lady would. Her dress was expensive, elegant, tasteful—from some little shop in New Orleans that imported the latest fashions from France, Howard surmised. He looked at the girl's dress. Yes, expensive. The eyes again? He was not sure. Irritably he cut across his steak with a vicious stroke, jiggling the crystal water goblet at his place. He quickly caught himself as Mrs. Todd glanced his way.

"Tell me," Father Reyneau continued his conversation with Mari. "Why is it so few Americans speak other languages, especially French, which is the language of the world?"

"Americans see little benefit in learning someone else's language when they can get them to speak theirs. However, we are not totally without skill. You've been in New Orleans. French is spoken there. In the West, there are many who speak at least some Spanish and Indian dialects. The street signs in San Antonio are posted in English, Spanish, and German." Mari ate her dinner without looking at Dr. Howard as he observed her from across the table.

"Ah, German, that is not language . . . that is mere grunting," protested the Frenchman.

114

"Still there are many Germans in Texas," Mari replied.

"Land," observed the Frenchman. "With Germans it is always the land they must own."

Joe Crites bent over his dinner, muttering to himself. "Well, Crites, you sat beside The Pagan and listened to her spend the evening talking in a foreign language to a sawed-off Frenchy."

Overhearing his mumbling, Mari smiled and touched his arm sympathetically, briefly.

Nothing seemed ever to be lost on Mrs. Todd. "To whom are you taking that dinner, young man?" she interrupted the table conversation as a young waiter passed toward the rear of the car with a silver domed tray protecting its steaming contents.

"To Mister Button, ma'am."

"Button is the chief porter," the woman said. "For whom is the tray intended?"

"I don't know that, ma'am. I just takes the tray to Mister Button." The young man continued to the rear of the car and gave the tray to the steward who headed toward the passenger car.

"Probably that hermit," Joe Crites speculated. "Man must be a reptile as hot as it is around his cabin. Have you noticed that? Every time I walk by there, it's hot as red coals."

"Has anyone seen this mystery passenger?" asked Mrs. Todd.

"It's not a mystery," replied Howard to dispel

115

the idle chitchat. "I believe he is an invalid, confined to a wheelchair. He entered the car just ahead of Boudinot."

"Well?" Mrs. Todd turned to Boudinot.

"I didn't see him," the lawyer said. "He was completely bundled up. I seem to remember he was wearing woolen gloves. Peculiar. Must be a medical condition or a disguise."

"Maybe he's like the soldier from Yuma who died and went to hell and came back that night to get a blanket because he was so cold," Crites chuckled.

"A medical condition," Mrs. Todd repeated, and studied Dr. Howard. "Is he your patient?"

"Not mine, ma'am. I'm a soldier's doctor generally."

"My husband was a soldier. Where did you serve in the late war, Doctor?"

"In Washington primarily. I worked in a special surgical unit and assisted the Sanitary Services in the hospitals there."

"You must have dealt with that Clara Barton. Tell me, what did you think of that horrible woman? Meddling and intrusive in what should be left to the men. My husband found her very difficult. You probably remember my husband, Brigadier General Omar Todd. A splendid officer taken long before his time. He found her extremely difficult in her demands for the men in the field. Really!"

"Missus Barton has, in her own way, changed medicine in this country," replied Howard. "Because of her sex, she was able to bring attention to problems that others could not. I do not think, in the future, we will see our wounded soldiers as neglected after the battles as they generally were before Miss Barton and the Sanitary Commission. I believe we understand now that we lost too many men as a result of our ignorance and arrogance. Too many were lost who could have lived with the proper care and sanitation."

"Just a lot of pampering more likely," muttered Mrs. Todd. "General Todd could not abide coddling his men . . . makes them weak and unreliable he always said. Your men must be more afraid of you than the enemy. They'll fight like men, then." Mari's head turned at the woman's harsh words. "That's what he always said."

"Men don't fight. Sometimes a man must fight a dog, but men don't fight. That's what my father said, and he, too, was a soldier," observed Mari. "Would you deny assistance to an injured man or comfort to a dying man, Missus Todd?" Mari studied the other woman. "I think not, Missus Todd. I suspect you hide a tender heart."

"Tender heart, rubbish! A war is not won by tending the wounded, but by attacking the enemy. These are things that are reckoned in waging war.

It has always been that way . . . for better or worse."

"And where were you and your high moral position, Miss Marshay, during the late war?" asked Phillip Howard.

Mari looked closely at the doctor. "I was in New Orleans part of the time."

"Comforting the Southern boys?" smirked Howard.

"When I could," answered Mari.

"You didn't neglect the Union boys, either, I trust. And after New Orleans?" pursued the doctor.

"I went West," Mari said.

"Why West?"

"Because I was sick of war and soldiers and death and dying, Doctor. What I saw surpassed my comprehension. I could not process the volume of suffering."

"You ran." Howard did not ask, he asserted. "Your father would have been very proud of you. Then what, Miss Marshay? Ah, I remember, you took up gambling."

"I had been gambling a long time before that, Doctor."

The other guests at the table held their knives and forks in mid-air as they listened to the quick, quiet, intense exchange between the man and woman. Neither Howard nor Mari Marshay seemed to realize there were others around them.

"Gambling's a vice, Miss Marshay," noted Howard, cutting his meat.

"So is surgery, Doctor, the way I saw it practiced."

Eli Boudinot's blue eyes studied Mari closely as she spoke.

"Life's a gamble," offered Joe Crites in a feeble effort to lighten the situation. "I mean every soldier knew it was fifty-fifty, live or die." He considered his words on hearing them for the first time. "Well, I guess some paid out. And there were some odds on being wounded so bad you'd be better off dead. I saw a guy once with an arm off one side and a leg off the other." He paused as he chewed. "Oh, it could have been worse. Could have been off the same side. Then, where'd the sucker be?"

"This is not table conversation," asserted Mrs. Todd, continuing her close observations and calculations on the relationship between the gambler and the doctor.

The diners shifted their attention to their food in silence. Taking a drink from the bead-frosted goblet at her setting, Mari began to regain the control she had briefly lost in the contest with Phillip Howard. She had not realized her temper and feelings lay so close to the surface. Perhaps the experiences of the last weeks, the travel had taken a toll on her nerves. Howard was nothing to her, merely something left behind long before this evening. Howard was nothing, Mari thought again. Still he irritated her. He always had. She must watch herself. That page was turned. She smiled at Susan Marn who sat very demurely and ate with both elegance and enthusiasm for the excellent cuisine. Jimmy Wing passed conspicuously toward the rear of the car with another tray hoisted aloft. His eyes were on Susan. When he caught Mari's eyes watching him, he winked.

"It's for Mister Marn, Missus Todd," he said brightly as he passed.

Her mouth drew into a straight thin line. "Servants should be invisible . . . neither seen nor *heard*. That is the proper way," Mrs. Todd stated, then picked up the thread of the earlier conversation. "My husband was a soldier. He knew how to do things properly. As he observed, war is simply a soldier's job. They are hired on to fight . . . whatever the risks. At its simplest, it is contractual. In return for their pay and food, they fight or work as the need be." Mrs. Todd nodded in affirmation. "At least the common soldier does. Officers generally find a higher motive, honor and country . . . service, all that."

Boudinot listened quietly, considering the words. "There are, of course, formation issues, meeting of minds being one . . . understanding of the terms another. Private agreements are made between private parties all the time. But a contract requires certain things. Our laws believe a man must understand clearly what is he is agreeing to. On the whole, few men understand how inconsequential their lives are to the generals or even to the medical professionals to whom they are ultimately given. Do you disagree with that, Doctor Howard?"

"Doctors are men, sir. They are also pushed to their limits in war. You have no idea what it is like to finish one surgery only to have another man laid before you and another and another for hours and even days."

"Almost as bad as being the man, I suppose," noted Boudinot dryly.

As the diners continued to pursue the great and small thoughts of mankind, *The Prairie Queen* cruised through the soft darkness. They dined contentedly, lingering over the specially prepared and served food in the handsomely appointed dining car.

"Father, can a man contract for his life?" asked Mari, turning to the man beside her and speaking in French.

"I should think as man has freedom to choose . . . he may choose what he does with his life." The priest did not look up from his meal as he answered softly.

"Father Reyneau thinks a man may contract for his life, just as Missus Todd says. What about you, Mister Beecher, in your faith can a man contract for his life?

"If a man cannot contract for his life," blurted Reverend Beecher, "he cannot be saved . . . for what else is salvation but the payment of one's old life and death for the gain of a new and eternal life."

"And here, Mister Beecher, can anyone give up his life simply for gain . . . say for food and pay?" asked Mari.

Leaning around his dinner partner, Beecher looked closely at the woman before he answered the question. "I suppose that could be . . . in an unconsidered way. A man with no resources would certainly be willing to exchange his services for food and pay. I doubt that he thinks much about his life being part of the bargain generally . . . except perhaps in the military in time of war."

"Is it a good bargain, Mister Beecher, the possibility of meager sustenance against the possibility of disease, dismemberment, or death?"

Howard joined the conversation. "In those terms the man would be simply exchanging one death from starvation for another from war. Not a very fine picture of mankind's great choices, eh, Mister Beecher?"

"We might say that death is inevitable, Doctor Howard," countered Beecher. "We are told very plainly that it is appointed once for all to die."

"If that were the case, and I believe it is, we are not choosing death at all, but a manner of life until such death inevitably comes," speculated Mari. "The Indians believe that. They live very close to death, depending on the fickleness of the natural world around them for their lives. They choose to deny death its power by facing it squarely and refusing to be afraid, often defying death by acts of bravery in battle."

"Ah, yes, your beloved Indian," Howard observed sarcastically. "White men don't think like that, Miss Marshay. We are interested in living, and I might add in living well."

"Amen, brother," said Joe Crites. "This isn't dinner conversation to soothe a stomach."

"Sorry," agreed Mari. "I got carried away on a speculative thought for which I am entirely unqualified, never having risked my fortune or my life as a soldier."

"You are right. You know nothing of men and war and their reasons and risks." Mrs. Todd nodded. "Women know nothing of the motives of men in war. But does a woman not also make a choice, a bargain for her life? When she marries, she ties her fortune to her husband's, perhaps her very life to bearing his children. That also is a dangerous choice with diverse motives. Can such a choice be made solely on attraction or even on need to have sustenance as someone said?"

"It has been my observation," Boudinot said, entering the conversation, "that very few decisions are made logically. Most people are totally unaware of choices. They simply act without thought, as a horse switches flies with its tail. For example, a man may rob a train with only the idea of getting easy money and tweaking the nose of the railroads. I doubt that he considers he may pay with years of his life or even with his life itself. People act without thought. Very little we do is based on conscious thought or choices that we understand. At least, that is true for the average man."

"I agree," said Phillip Howard. "There is very little conscious thought in life. We respond to stimuli."

"What stimuli? Why?" asked Mari.

"Whatever comes our way. Because it relieves some pressure and meets our momentary need," responded Howard.

"Oh, Doc,"—Mari smiled—"you don't believe that."

"I certainly do believe that," Howard insisted.

"I believe that we do choose," Beecher said quietly. "Perhaps not in every moment, perhaps not even every man, but some men consciously choose. Even in the multiplicity of life, there is only one set of choices. They choose good or bad."

"Really, who is to know good or bad, sir?" asked Boudinot. "As a lawyer, I have seen an innocent choice lead to disastrous consequences. Take your faith, a woman chose a simple apple in the hope that it would enrich her life, not destroy it. Hence, the fall of mankind . . . the great Biblical curse. Good and bad are all relative."

Mari considered Boudinot's face, a mask, now, protecting the ebullient man of the afternoon.

"We have put so much emphasis on that poor choice and its sinful results that we often fail to consider a second choice and its liberating consequences," Beecher said. "Reconciliation is a choice offered to us, promised from the beginning, but neglected because of our fascination with eternal punishment, fire and brimstone . . . the verity of fear as General Todd believed. If we cannot persuade with gently offering our Christ for choice, we place our thumb on the scale and tip it with the fear of unbearable judgment and anguish beyond death. To be fully human, we must choose and know the choice and its consequences . . . good or bad. We cannot let life make our decisions. We must make them." Beecher was speaking softly again.

"And how do we know what to choose, Mister Beecher? What is the basis?" asked Mari. "To relieve pressure, to meet our momentary needs?"

"Oh, no." The cleric shook his head, looking at his plate. "Our only standard must be love."

"Yes," observed Boudinot with a slight smirk. "I've found a respite of love often relieves the pressure quite well."

"In my work, I many times become caught up in

the chaos of the mundane," admitted Beecher. "I see mankind's pettiness and sins, the thoughtless acts that pull men down. I fall back on rules. I look at the choices and condemn the man. I am disappointed in our species." He nodded at Phillip Howard, the scientist. "And in myself. But I think very few things matter except the single choice to love God and my fellow creatures. All my acts are ultimately measured against that choice to love. I succeed or fail by my constancy to that choice. That is the substance of a life."

The French priest touched Mari's arm, and she turned to him. He spoke to her in his language. "Mademoiselle, I often understand English better than I can convey a thought. I think this clergyman might use a phrase from Saint Francis of Assisi. Do you know the one I mean?"

Mari's brow furrowed in thought. "When we fight for the love of truth, we should not forget the truth of love?"

"Yes," whispered Reyneau.

Boudinot sighed. "I'm not inclined to verities. We live. We die. All this is too deep for a hot night in the middle of the Nations. Here, there is no substance, only shadow. That is worthy of our fear."

"We do not fear the shadow of a dog, Mister Boudinot," said Mari. "We fear his substance."

As the waiters cleared away the last crumbs of the dessert, the passengers began to push back from the damask-covered table. In three short blasts the whistle cried out the approach of the final water stop in the Choctaw Division of the Missouri, Kansas, and Texas Railroad.

"Must be McAlester," observed Crites.

Young Jimmy Wing heard the same signal as he scrubbed the stove in the galley of the car. He rested on the black iron, thinking.

"Boy, you ain't finished," the chef said.

"No sir, I ain't, but I got to see to something when the train stops. Then I'll finish up."

The thin cook sighed. What could he do with one assistant sick and the substitute preoccupied? You made do. You made do.

The engineer lay down on the whistle, a long steady blast, as the station came into sight. *The Prairie Queen* slowed perceptibly, coasting into the water stop. *The Queen*, being a first class or limited, had avoided many stops and technicalities of the transportation system. Most trains, however, especially the lower priority ones, on the Katy line stopped at ten-mile intervals to refill the small tenders. The frequent and necessary stops were also good business for the Katy. They meant freight and passengers from the towns that grew around the line. Normally, being a land grant railroad, the Katy would also have had the lucrative right to sell lots in the towns to the people they enticed West, like the immigrants in the forward cars. Levi Parsons, founder of the line, considered the land his, and used it as a lever to obtain financing for its building. However, the Five Civilized Tribes had put a stop to his dream, contending that the land was theirs by treaty and that the government could not give away land that did not belong to them. The Indians had learned some things about white men and their laws and were using that knowledge to force the issue to the Supreme Court.

At McAlester, the main line of the Katy branched off toward Krebs and Wilburton and their coal mines. The immigrants would be re-routed here to the final destination on their overland journey. The branch line at McAlester supplied most of the coal used by the Katy locomotives.

At McAlester, the train crew and engine would change and another engine and crew would replace them to take the train on through the Cherokee Division and into Parsons, Kansas. The Choctaw Division engine would be serviced and prepared for its trip back to Denison. Its crew, having worked its ten hours and two hundred and fifty miles, would go home. However, the men assigned to the care of the passengers in the presidential car would remain.

Crites drew back the velvet drapery to clear his view of the proceedings outside. "Looks like they're going to uncouple the immigrant cars," he observed. "I bet this takes longer than an hour. Well, maybe we'll make it up. Go in express without the extra cars. Wonder how we rated a deal like that?" The man braced his stubby hands against the table. "Gents, it's about time for a good cigar in the open air? Say, Miss Marshay, when we get back under way, how about a friendly game of cards to pass the time."

Mari replaced her napkin and smiled. "Sorry, Mister Crites. I don't play cards any more. I've passed enough time."

"Well,"—Crites winked, laying down his napkin—"call me Joe anyway."

As the men started to rise, the rear door of the dining car opened, revealing a tall, mustached man. Light from the ceiling chandelier caught and bounced off the badge pinned to his vest. A shotgun rested casually in the curve of his left elbow. "Ladies and gents, bring some identification and come outside onto the platform."

Chapter Ten

For a long moment, the diners sat quietly considering the lawman's words. "What's this all about?" Beecher queried.

"This is the Nations," Boudinot said. "And that is a United States deputy marshal out of the Fifth Circuit of the Western District of Arkansas. They are looking for someone, I would guess. I certainly hope he had sense enough to get into the brush."

As a gambler, Mari had learned to read slight nuisances in the other players—the lifting of an eyebrow, a nervous flicker in a finger. She noted a hardness and tension in Boudinot's voice that had not been there that afternoon on the swaying platform.

Not hearing or unsatisfied with the strange man's explanation, Mrs. Todd asked Beecher: "What do you think it is?"

"I'm sure I do not know. But perhaps it is as Boudinot suggests . . . the marshals are looking for a wrongdoer," Beecher postulated.

"Wrongdoer?" Mrs. Omar Todd's voice pitched up shrilly.

"I'll bet they're looking for a murderer or train robber," Joe Crites speculated to Mrs. Todd. "Nothing less would bring 'em out like this."

"I do not bet, sir," the woman huffed. "Murderer!"

With the deputy marshal stoically watching, the passengers began leaving the table and returning to their own compartments to gather the requested identification.

Mari returned Susan Marn, quickly, to her father's compartment. She caught a glimpse of Jimmy Wing, who had been painstakingly attentive to their needs at the table all evening, as he was exiting the car. "Jimmy, will you help Mister Marn and his daughter while I get my things."

The boy hesitated. "I've got to do something right now," he began.

Susan smiled at him. "We'll manage," she assured Jimmy and Mari.

"No," the boy melted. "I'll help you. I can watch from there."

"Watch what?"

"Stuff," the boy replied absently as he followed Susan.

Mari smiled to herself at his pathetic infatuation as she went to her own cubicle. How wonderful to be young and in love. As she paused at the door, the smile faded. Not so wonderful sometimes, she remembered.

One by one the passengers descended from *The Prairie Queen* onto the platform of the new brick dépôt. When they had assembled, the deputy marshal who had entered the train began to examine them individually. He looked closely at each man, then at the identification offered.

"I bet you're looking for a murderer," Joe Crites suggested as the officer studied his papers.

The deputy marshal looked at Crites's face. "You like to bet on things . . ."—he checked the papers again—"Mister Crites?"

"That's right," agreed Crites. "Betting is just a way of looking at things, I suppose. Keeps you interested in what's going on around you, gives you a little stake in the events. So who is it you're looking for?"

"A badman," said the deputy marshal without commitment as he moved on.

Crites's face showed the disappointment he felt at not having gotten the inside information. He shifted the cigar, clamping his jaw.

"Doctor Howard?" the deputy marshal asked, after reading the offered identification.

"Yes," Howard said.

"Fort Sill?" pursued the deputy marshal.

"Actually, I was in Texas," said Howard mildly.

The deputy marshal folded the document and handed it back to the doctor.

The Reverend Beecher handed across his papers as the lawman stopped before him. "Really, Marshal, you've dragged us all away from our evening meal. An explanation couldn't hurt. Obviously it is not one of us. None of us is an outlaw. We are all law-abiding men with substantial means without resorting to robbery, or whatever." An unpleasant thought hit the

132

minister. "You're not looking for a woman, I trust."

"Just a tip," the deputy marshal said, handing back the papers. "The man we're looking for might be on this train. Outlaws pretty much have it their own way once they get into the Nations. For us to get involved there must be a crime against a white man or his property by an Indian, or *vice versa*. The Indians handle their own problems among themselves, their courts. This time we were tipped about a suspect . . . got our writ . . . got here."

Boudinot offered his papers in a leather wallet. The deputy marshal opened it without taking his eyes off Boudinot's dark face.

Boudinot did not avert his eyes, but met the lawman's steadily. He showed no defiance.

"Your business, sir?"

"Attorney," replied Boudinot.

"Interesting business," the deputy marshal observed, placing the wallet in Boudinot's hand and looking directly into his eyes. "Officer of the court."

Boudinot's heavily lidded eyes held the lawman's. "Yes," he smiled. "We're in the same business, you and I."

The deputy marshal smiled. "But you are on the money end, not me."

He finished with the other men methodically and moved to the women beside Joshua Marn.

Again he followed form, asking name and occupation and confirming it with the paper each offered and his instinct of what each should be.

"What business are you in, Missus Todd?" he asked the woman before him.

"I'm not in any business, young man. I am a respectable widow. My husband was General Omar Todd."

The officer of the court smiled as he looked down at his boots, then handed back the papers. Moving on to the next woman, he took the papers and read. "Miss Marshay?"

"That's right."

"Do you have an occupation, Miss Marshay?" The deputy marshal studied her thoughtfully, observing the expensive clothing and jewelry and the carriage of the woman.

"I'm a pilgrim," Mari responded.

"And where are you bound, Miss Marshay?" The lawman lingered before the woman.

Before Mari could answer, a scuffle down the track at an immigrant car caused him to quickly hand back her identification. His hand checked the big sidearm laced against his leg. He went to his men.

Watie Boudinot, Beecher's 'breed from the afternoon tour of the cars, struggled between two deputies. He kicked and twisted, cursed profusely.

"I'll kill the son-of-a-bitch who spilled his guts

to the law," Watie swore, fighting the strong men who held him.

"Shut up," the deputy marshal said quietly.

The 'breed spat into the deputy marshal's mustache. Without hesitation the deputy marshal's pistol slid into his hand and came down across the outlaw's head. He slumped in the arms of the deputies.

"Take him on," the lawman said, holstering his weapon and wiping the spittle from his face with an already grimy handkerchief. He turned back to the passengers watching from the platform. "That's all we'll need, folks. You can go back in now. Sorry for the delay."

The small group of men and women from the presidential car headed back and slowly boarded.

"I really do not think he had to be so violent with that man," Beecher said. "There were, after all, three of them. What could one man do against three?"

"Saved him time, I suppose," offered Phillip Howard. The doctor allowed Mrs. Todd to board ahead of him as he finished his cigar. "Sometimes it's best to get something unpleasant over quickly."

Howard watched as Susan and Jimmy Wing guided the old mountain man up the steps and into the car. He hesitated, thinking, then gave Mari his hand, helped her onto the step. "Mister Marn's

Cheyenne daughter," he smiled confidently, sure of his observation.

Mari looked back at him from the iron platform and at Beecher behind him. "You need to get out of your surgery more, Doc," the woman noted, and moved into the car. Dr. Howard and Beecher followed.

"Where's Boudinot?" asked Joe Crites as he turned back at the top step.

"*Pardon, m'sieu, je ne parle pas anglais*," the French cleric responded.

"Aw, shoot!" sputtered Crites. "I'm getting mighty tired of you, Frenchy."

"*Oui, m'sieu*," the priest agreed politely.

Inside the telegraph office Boudinot's large hand rested on the small paper telegraphic form as he studied his message. The penmanship was clear and well-disciplined. He crossed out a word and replaced it with another. He glanced quickly out the window, noting that the passengers were again boarding *The Prairie Queen*.

"Send this at once," Boudinot said to the brass-pounder. He laid the money for the telegram and a tip on the counter. "No change." The boy nodded his thanks and sat down at the key. Boudinot paced the office, looking out the window as the message streaked over the thin wire across the black night. "Come on, come on," he said softly to himself.

"They got it, sir." The telegrapher stood up from the metal key. "There's an answer. You want to wait for it?"

"I know the reply." Boudinot closed the door behind him before the telegrapher had stated the final word of his question. He returned to the train and slipped onto the stairway as the Frenchman entered the coach.

The key called the telegrapher's attention away from the man boarding the train. He sat down and wrote out the return message. It said simply: **Will do**. The boy wadded the paper and tossed it into the waste can as *The Prairie Queen* moved again toward the darkness.

Chapter Eleven

The Prairie Queen moved through the night, clicking rhythmically over the rails. In truth, no city knows a night as black as the moonless prairie night that embraced her. It was as if the world itself had been entirely extinguished and replaced once again by the primordial void. The train clung to the rails lit only by her single headlight. To step to right or left meant nothingness, endless, bottomless nothingness. To leave the Indian bridge of iron, the fragile filament linking civilization to civilization across the unknown country, meant plunging into a sea of unknown darkness.

But inside the cabin of the brightly lit car, the passengers rode unmindful of the dark world that surrounded them. Stewards moved through the compartments, preparing them for their residents' slumber as the passengers lingered in the small lounge. The incident with the lawmen and their prisoner had disturbed the expected routine of a leisurely dinner followed by a long and comfortable sleep. In short, the travelers had been interrupted and needed the company of the others before easing again into their private worlds.

"Thought we'd lost you back there at the station," chatted Crites as Boudinot joined the others in the lounge.

Boudinot smiled. His eyes twinkled with a peculiar fire. "You'll never lose me . . . not yet, anyway."

"Well, what was that all about?" exclaimed Mrs. Todd, dropping uncharacteristically onto a tufted couch. "My word, I never expected to be scrutinized by the law while riding with the line president's own entourage. Is that what traveling has sunk to?"

"It's the West, Missus Todd," explained Reverend Beecher. "I've been traveling in the West for several years now. I can tell you the least you can expect is to be discomfited and uncomfortable even when things are going well."

"Whatever happened to patience and forbearance?" queried Phillip Howard.

"That wears very thin in the West," answered Beecher. "But I've never been taken from the train like a common criminal. Nor have I seen the needlessly violent capture of a man before."

"New England man, eh?" Crites face was flushed from the excitement, but he testified. "That was nothing. Just an outlaw taken by the authorities. I saw two men kill each other dead over a game of cards in Texas. One minute peacefully playing. The next dead as mackerels. Life can turn on a dime out here. You saw the shooting, lady." He turned to Mari Marshay for confirmation.

Boudinot casually watched the woman's response.

Mari lowered her eyes thoughtfully, then brought them back to Crites's face. "Yes, I saw it. Two men dead for nothing."

"Nothing but a pile of money," countered Crites.

"Yes, that's right . . . nothing but money."

"Greed and avarice," sputtered Reverend Beecher, studying the woman closely, unsure of her true character. "Unchanged human nature is not a pretty picture."

"Well, that's a pretty picture," Crites observed, gesturing at the painting that dominated the lounge. "Art is a mystery to me, but *that* is a pretty picture. That's a proud, noble-looking woman. I suppose the artist colored that up some, romanticized her. When you look at things realistically, the hard life, the struggle for their daily bread, the abuse by their men, I don't reckon there are too many Indian women that really look like that."

"I cannot see the picture, sir," said Marn. "But I can tell you that there are many beautiful Indian women. I'm married to three of them."

Mrs. Todd closed her eyes tightly as her thin lips pursed. But she said nothing.

"My daughter here is also beautiful."

"She is only half Indian," observed Phillip Howard.

"The better half, sir," responded Josh Marn.

"Say, Boudinot, what are you?" Crites asked suddenly. "I mean, are you a white man, or what?"

"My mother was white. My father mostly Cherokee," Boudinot said.

Crites scrutinized the face. Boudinot was well-featured with an angular nose, high cheek bones, a square chin, and a light copper skin that suggested healthful outdoor living. His dark hair appeared black. But on a closer look, without the grooming oil he wore, it would have been lighter, as much brown as black. His hair was long for a white man, romantic like some of the frontiersmen and poets wore. It hung full and straight above his immaculate white collar. A white shirt in the West proved he was not a man who worked with his hands. His eyes beneath the heavy lids and dark lashes were a penetrating blue. A handsome man, Crites concluded, but there was an unsettling trace of the uncivilized, even savage, glazing the good looks.

"Ain't it usually the other way around?" Crites's words followed his thoughts.

"My mother was a Philadelphia liberal with a passion for causes and my father," Boudinot answered.

"You sure look white," said Crites.

"I'm not proud of my white blood," Boudinot stated without animosity or bitterness. "I suspect the child will not be, either." He looked gently at Susan Marn, who blushed under his gaze and attention.

"Shoot!" exclaimed Crites. "I don't know why. What's the percentage in being an Indian? Hell, man, the newspapers are even callin' the Indian Mister 'Lo, as in 'lo, the poor Indian. It's a white man's world, brother."

"Really?" Boudinot said, turning to the window and the blackness beyond. "A white man's world? That's an interesting concept when we are in the Nations."

"Ladies," the porter announced. "Your compartments are prepared."

"Well, at last," huffed Mrs. Todd, struggling to her feet. "An end to this day and its irritations. I hope that Louisey has not forgotten to put out my valerian drops."

"I'm sure she has not," Mari said as she stood to follow. Mari knew Louise was smart enough to want to provide any herb that would relax Mrs. Todd and cause her to sleep soundly.

"Go ahead, child." Josh Marn nodded to his daughter. "I will stay and have a drink with the men before I come to the room."

Mari Marshay waited to allow the girl to proceed her.

"Hum. Anyway, maybe we can get some rest now. Good night." Mrs. Todd's voice trailed off as she disappeared.

Down the hall, Susan Marn hesitated. "Do you think Father will be all right?"

"He crossed an uncharted continent," said Mari. "He can find his way down this little hall."

"But he was young, and he could see, and times were different."

Jimmy Wing appeared from the platform end of the corridor. He smiled quickly, accommodatingly. "I'll see Mister Marn gets any help he needs, Miss Marn. Good night, ladies."

"Good night, Mister Wing," the young girl said, as Jimmy slowly passed her on his way back to the lounge. He walked very tall and straight in his white jacket.

" 'Good night, sweet prince.' " Mari smiled to herself as she entered her small room, then she had an idea. "Susan, I'm just starting a book by Wilkie Collins. Would you like to read together until your father returns?"

"Oh, yes, that would be nice. I need to practice my reading."

"Good. Then you shall read aloud, and I shall listen."

Once they were inside the compartment, Mari slipped into her chair and handed the book to Susan Marn. The girl took it and opened the volume as she sat near the lamp. " 'This is the story of what a woman's patience can endure, and what a man's resolution can achieve,' " she began.

● ● ●

After the women had departed, the men lingered idly, awaiting the porter's call that their rooms, too, were prepared for the night. Jimmy Wing opened the well-furnished liquor cabinet and began to set out glasses and cigars for the men. He handed the cigars to Crites.

Beecher seemed restless. "I think I'll get some air before I turn in. This has been a most confusing day." He went toward the front platform.

"Bourbon all around?" Crites asked the others, tossing the cigars before placing one in Josh Marn's large hand. "How about you, Frenchy? You understand . . . bourbon?"

"*Oui, m'sieur,*" said the little priest, leaning forward and catching the Havana. Around him the others nodded their affirmation to the drink as they settled deeply into the comfortable chairs. Jimmy Wing began filling the glasses and serving them carefully to the passengers.

Leaning back against the small bar, Crites picked up a cigar, sniffed it, and rolled it between his finger and thumb near his ear. He tasted the amber liquid set before him and audibly sighed. "This is a pleasant end to a hectic day. Very pleasant. A game or two of cards would have been the capper. I'd like to have said I sat down at a poker table with The Pagan. Too bad she's given up the game. But I guess she had a pretty bad scare in Texas. Probably figures her luck has run out."

Phillip Howard drew deeply on the cigar and exhaled a plume of smoke into the air. He grimly studied the toe of his boot.

"How'd you know The Pagan, Doctor Howard?" asked Crites.

Howard looked up at the round, little man. He hesitated, considering the man's question and his own answer. "I don't know this *Pagan*. I was in Miss Marshay's father's regiment, his assistant surgeon."

"So what's the scandal? What happened to make her The Pagan?"

"I'm sure I have no idea," answered Howard. "But for her father's sake, if not her own, I will not discuss her for idle curiosity's sake. And please do not use that name, The Pagan, in my presence. It is offensive and does neither her nor her father any good." The doctor rose to his feet. "If you will excuse me, gentlemen, I've some reading to catch up on. Good night."

Boudinot's eyes followed Howard across the salon and into the passage leading back to his compartment.

Joe Crites whistled softly. "Well, that was pretty straight, wasn't it? Touchy sort of fellow."

"Touchy, yes," agreed Boudinot, drawing on the cigar. "But why?"

"Well, I meant nothing offensive. I just figured

145

there was a reason for a quality woman like that getting that name. I never intended to insult her . . . or him."

"Sometimes men are peculiar about the women they love," observed Josh Marn.

"Indeed," Boudinot confirmed, sipping his whisky. "For a blind man, you see a great deal."

"Yes, Mister Boudinot, sometimes a blind man can see what a seeing man does not," agreed the old man.

Crites leaned his elbow on the bar, looking at the painting of the "Prairie Queen." "I still say it's a pretty picture. It's a pretty picture, sure enough."

The men smoked contentedly and drank the bonded bourbon with appreciation as the train moved through the night.

The porter and steward reappeared when their tasks were completed. "Gentlemen," the porter said, and simply gestured toward their cabins.

"Well, looks like we can turn in now." Crites set his glass on the polished wood table. Placing his hands on his knees, he raised his rotund body and headed eagerly toward his bed.

Boudinot watched him go, and put down his own glass. His eyes ran over the now nearly empty salon. Only Marn, the French priest, and Jimmy Wing remained. "Can I show you to your compartment, Mister Marn?" the lawyer offered.

"I'll see that Mister Marn gets home," Jimmy

Wing said quickly. "I told his daughter I would."

"Good night, then." Boudinot nodded. "Until next time, gentlemen."

Jimmy Wing put away the glasses, closed and locked the bar. "Whenever you are ready, Mister Marn."

The old man rose to his full height and placed his hand on the youth's shoulder. "Take me home, son. I am weary."

"*Bon nuit*," the priest nodded to Boudinot, and rose to follow young Jimmy Wing and the venerable mountain man.

"Good night, sir," said Boudinot. The handsome 'breed remained seated, smoking his cigar thoughtfully, listening to the others depart for their bedchambers.

Hearing the men in the aisle, Mari interrupted Susan's reading. "Your father's coming, I think."

"Well," the girl rose quickly, handing the book to Mari. "Good night, Miss Marshay. It's a very exciting book."

Mari held the book to her chest as the girl went into the hall. She heard Jimmy open the door and escort Josh Marn across the platform into the passenger car beyond. Jimmy returned to the door just as Susan was saying her good night to Mari. They stood for a long moment just being close. Mari looked down, then rose and closed the door, smiling her own pleasant thoughts. She stood a long time with the book in her arms, leaning against the door, remembering when just being close to someone was enough. Finally she tossed the book on the bed and began to undress.

When the steward returned to put out the lights, Boudinot ground out the last ember of his cigar and strolled toward the rear of the car. Phillip Howard's door was closed. As Boudinot passed, the light within was extinguished. "It's a white man's world," he whispered, and smiled to himself. He continued to the platform beyond. His hand upon the guardrail, he rocked gently with the rhythm of *The Prairie Queen* as she slid over the white man's cold steel rails, crossing the living Nations. Boudinot could hear the land, feel it pulsing in the darkness. He studied the stars, nodding to them as to old friends, friends with Cherokee names as ancient as the People could remember. "It's not a white man's world . . . not all of it, not here," he whispered to the listening land. Boudinot drew a small pistol from his waist, checked the load, and then casually replaced the weapon. He smiled. "They only think it's a white man's world." He chuckled to himself. "Comes the great awakening."

Chapter Twelve

Mari Marshay could not read for drowsing and could not sleep for awakening. She sat up on the side of the bed, pushing her hands through her hair. "Damn," she said, and sighed. She put on the robe, lying over the chair arm, and her slippers, then went into the hall. She stood for a moment without direction or purpose other than to be out of the tumbled bed. Finally she walked toward the lounge. A half light revealed the painting of the "Prairie Queen" in the dark room. The image of the noble Indian woman drew her across the floor. She stood in front of the painting, reached out to touch the surface, hoping the red pigment would be warm to her fingers. She smiled suddenly at her own foolishness before the illusion created by daubs of paint on linen. Feeling another presence, she turned to search the darkness.

"Phillip?"

"Why did you do it?" asked Howard from a heavy chair.

"I had the silly idea the paint would actually feel warm to my fingers."

"No, why did you go off with them . . . with the damned buck?"

Mari sat on the arm of his chair. She looked softly at Phillip who studied his boot toe intently.

"Don't do that," he said. As she started to rise, his hand caught her wrist and held her. "It's not fair. Tell me why you went off for four days with an Apache buck. Why you came back bold as brass down the middle of the parade ground with yellow pollen all over you?"

"Maybe I didn't know I did anything wrong, anything that should warrant my slipping about."

He twisted to face her. "Oh, come on, now, Mari. You were a pretty big girl not to know what we all thought."

"I can never be responsible for what you thought, Phillip. Not you. Not anyone else. I'm only responsible for my actions and what I think of myself. I did not think I had done anything that I had to explain."

"Good God Almighty!" Howard jumped to his feet. "Four days, Mari. We hunted everywhere."

"I am sorry about that." She slid from the chair arm into the seat. "I left a note."

"Nobody ever saw a note, Mari." Howard paced in front of her.

"That was a hundred years ago, Phillip," she said flatly. "I did not feel I had to explain then, and I do not feel I have to explain now."

"I wanted to be able to trust you, Mari." Howard's pacing slowed. There was a catch in his voice. "A man has to trust the woman who is to be his wife."

"Then you should have trusted me."

"It wasn't a game, Mari. It was our life together, and you threw it away."

"Did I?" she asked wistfully. "Did I throw it away, Phillip, all by myself?" She rested her head against the back of the chair. "Perhaps I did. It was so long ago. It seemed so important then that you trusted me . . . believed I would not do anything to hurt you."

"Hurt me, Mari? You tore out my heart. I loved you, wanted you to be my wife, and you didn't think enough of that to . . ." The doctor paused.

"To what Phillip? Tell you the truth. I wanted you to already know the truth . . . that I loved you, that I would not deceive you or be unfaithful to you ever."

"You deceived me that afternoon at the river. Oh, you were coy, refusing me, holding me off so you could go with that savage. There I've said it. You seduced or were seduced by a savage, a stone age animal, on the eve of our wedding. You came back from that little tryst a different woman than I knew."

Mari smiled at the man standing above her with his hands on his hips. She stood up, saying: "You're always too high up and too far away."

"Why couldn't you just tell me nothing happened?" he implored.

"Nothing happened." Mari smiled, pushing back the shock of hair that had fallen across his face. Her hand lingered on his jaw.

151

"We've lost so many years. Could we ever get them back?"

"I don't know, Doc. There's something missing between us. Maybe we have different expectations, too." Mari's fingers caressed his face. He kissed her palm hungrily.

"Have there been many men, Mari?"

She looked into his earnest face, then looked away. "I've never done anything I was ashamed of." She paused, appearing to think about her past. "Well, there was that time in the Rockies when I over wintered with three miners."

"Mari," moaned Howard.

She looked directly into his eyes. "I made that up, Doc."

"Games," he whispered. "Be serious, Mari."

"I am serious. But something about you, about us . . . maybe you are so serious I can't be."

"Have there been many men, Mari?" he repeated softly.

"Not a one, Doc." She smiled, feeling the warmth of his nearness.

"I believe you," he said, drawn to her, wanting to believe her.

"You'd better not, Doc."

Phillip Howard began to draw away, to stand back. Then he stopped and reached for Mari. "I believe you, Mari."

One hand reached out to straighten his collar as the other familiarly circled his waist. "Not yet,

Doc." She turned gently around him and moved away back into the passage as his hand almost reached out. "Good night, Phillip."

Howard sat down quickly, burying his head in his hands with consternation. "Damn," he muttered.

In the shadows of the aisle, the ember of Boudinot's cigar flared, then disappeared into the darkness. The platform door opened without a sound, and he stepped outside. Drawing deeply on the cigar, he leaned back against the wall and stared out into the passing darkness. The remembered voices, the movement in the half darkness of the lounge reverberated in his mind, awakening the thoughts of another time.

"Dead. Dead. Dead." The words, paced by short pauses, were faint and distant as the lantern bobbed through the darkness. Boudinot was cold, colder than he had ever been. It was a cold from within, his shivering body allowing the inner warmth to dissipate into the wet ground fog. "Dead." The indifferent voice was nearer now. "Dead. Dead." The lantern swung into Boudinot's eyes as the triage walked past. He could not move enough even to blink at the brightness that hid the face above him. "Dead." The lantern moved on.

"Wait," a softer voice said. "This man is not dead."

"Dead," said the other, moving away in the darkness.

"No," the woman's soft voice spoke again. "This man is alive."

The lantern stopped moving away. "He is dead . . . or will be in a short time. We cannot waste time on the hopeless. Come, woman."

The woman kneeled above Boudinot. Her fingers moved into the collar of his blood-splattered tunic. At the light touch on his throat, he felt something jerk inside him. The heat stopped flowing out of him. The cold stopped entering.

"Leave that man at once," the man's voice, distant, barked at the woman.

"No," Boudinot struggled to say through lips too thick with death and cold to form the word. He could not see the woman. Boudinot was blind from the shell that had burst in his face, that had sent fragments ripping through his body and brought him to the stone pavement of the makeshift hospital. She placed her hand on his chest very gently, very surely. He understood it to be some kind of promise as she covered him with her long cape. Then she was gone into the night and fog. He slipped again into unconsciousness.

Some time later, there were big hands under

his shoulders, jerking him up from the wet stones. Someone had his feet. He glimpsed the shadow of a black face above him. *Oh, God,* Boudinot thought, *they are going to bury me. They are going to throw me alive into the pit and cover me, smother me with dirt.* He tried to speak, to tell them he was alive. But nothing moved, no sound came forth. His body was encased, cocooned, in coming death. Then the warm and gentle hand, the strong and sure hand, was there again on his cheek.

They carried him through the night. They entered a building and laid him on a table in a damp room that smelled of blood and sweat, of urine and body waste, of carbolic.

"Jeter, give me the blankets," the woman said to the black man, and then covered Boudinot with the warmth. He smelled her, felt the heat of her body drawing him back, not in false desire, but in an attempt to fulfill his need for life-verifying warmth. There was light now all around him. She was in the light. Although he could not see her, she was there. He felt her presence. They slowly stripped away his wet, gore-soaked garments, and washed him with warm water. He was becoming clean. She rubbed his arms and chest, his legs, his feet with towels, taking away the wetness and cold, covering the returning warmth with the blankets, holding the warmth to him so that it could not escape. There was pain, too, small sharp pain. It seemed inconsequential, trivial, somewhere on the edge of his consciousness, thorns being pulled from his body. A hand touched his forehead. He realized that the woman was the pain, the healing pain taking the shell fragments from his wounds, the healing pain of the needle piercing his flesh and sewing it back together. He breathed, shivering again. More blankets were put over him. At last, she lay down against his large body, infusing it with the living warmth of her own small being. Boudinot drifted away, resting, trusting the warmth, the woman, swimming toward her back from death.

When he awoke, she was gone. She did not come again.

There were men's voices now. The men lifted him from the table and carried him somewhere in the dark room to a cot. They did not take away the blankets.

For days Boudinot slept and woke in the New Orleans ward. He caught the hands of those that tended him, but they were not the woman's. Finally he could ask: "Where is the woman?"

"What woman?" his disinterested attendant asked.

"The woman!" Boudinot shouted, as if the intensity of his words would make his meaning clear.

But the woman was never there.

The weeks passed, the bandages were removed from Boudinot's eyes. He could look out onto the courtyard where he had lain that night in the fog and rain as the doctor passed from body to body, sorting the quick and the dead. It was once a pretty place with old stone pavers and plants that bloomed in the moist heat and shaded the place from the harsh sun. Now the plants, neglected, had gone to jungle. Now there were piles of refuse burning slowly on the stones.

"Jeter," a voice called out from somewhere inside.

Boudinot turned to see a black man walking though the building. Boudinot staggered to his feet, holding the wall. He hastened after the man. "Wait," he called out in a voice he did not recognize.

The big black stopped. "Whatchuwant, sir?"

"The woman," Boudinot blurted. "Where is the woman?"

The man's smooth face slid into a frown. "Ain't no woman here, sir."

"Please," Boudinot whispered desperately. "You helped her. You carried me in . . . you and another man. She saved my life."

157

The black man looked about quickly. "Don't say nuffin' 'bout that, boss. Not so old doc kin hear you. That woman, she got in trouble for what she done that night . . . for takin' things on herself, crossin' the doctor, actin' like she's the doctor when she weren't. I ain't seen no man madder than old doc, not even in the fields when some nigger driver beatin' somebody. He yellin' so loud warn't nobody miss his words but the long dead. Say he only put up wif her 'cause of her pappy. He call the laws on her. She never told 'bout me and Tiny helpin'. She tell old doctor he weren't nuffin' but a butcher. That what she say. 'You ain't nuffin' but a butcher pretending to be a phyz-ian.' Little woman like that talkin' right up in old doc's whiskers. She ain't skeered of nuffin'. She right, too. I does the burin' here . . . sometimes too many to bury, some just cut open and left like they wuz, like a butcher pen for animals not men. When she wuz here, at least she sew 'em back together."

Boudinot sank toward the foot of a cot. The great black hand caught him and eased him down. "What was her name? Where did she go?"

The black man seemed puzzled. "Don't know, sir. Just call her Missy. She never come back after the laws took her out. Nobody tell a nigger nuffin'."

Chapter Thirteen

Three Forks Station, Indian Territory

The telegram arrived at the Three Forks Station long before *The Prairie Queen* would have to stop there for water. The rough, unpainted, board station took its name from the ancient site where three rivers—the Arkansas, the Grand, and the Verdigris—ran together. White men and Indians had traded here when the Arkansas was a principal means of transport into the dark unknown interior of the North American continent. Their small boats had tied up under the bluff. They had walked up on hard young legs to barter trinkets for fur and the softness of the Indian women.

The first Cherokees had come into this country in an effort to rid themselves of the white man, voluntarily removing themselves from his presence to the promised lands in the West—an emerald in the hollow of the Ozark Plateau and its mountains. They were the pure-bloods then, not confused in heritage or ambition. All they wanted was the land and what it offered. But later other Cherokees, many with mixed-blood, were forced out of their old lands, Andrew Jackson simply refusing to enforce the right to their lands in North Carolina and Georgia. So, in 1838, these Cherokees made the long sad march to the

West—The Trail of Tears. Every mile had broken their hearts with the deaths of their people, their old and their young, and with the knowledge of their betrayal by their white friends and by their own leaders. Many of these Indians were more white than red, men like John Ridge, only a sixteenth Cherokee, who had signed away their country to the white men. Ridge had, of course, paid for his crime. He and his compatriots had been stabbed or axed to death in their new homes by the vengeful hands of those who did not wish to give the white men their land.

This was in the dark land of the Nations of betrayed men. The five tribes from the East—Cherokee, Choctaw, Chickasaw, Seminole, and Creek—each took a portion of the new land, each established its own government with officers and courts, but each remembered the old country, their home before the white man. Each carried the knowledge, reinforced by the muffled beat of their own hearts, that flowing within their own veins was now a secret white man—mentor, friend, betrayer.

The full-bloods said that the trouble with a mixed-blood was that one day he was white and the next he was red. He was never the same. He was untrustworthy. He was not an Indian always. He did not want the same things. The mixed-bloods said the trouble with the pure-bloods was that they lacked initiative. They did not have the decisiveness to go forward on the white man's road. If there were three full-bloods considering a course of action, the mixed-bloods said, there would be four opinions on what to do.

Many Indian daughters married white men who courted these girls for their beauty, but also for the farming land they could put under plow without paying for it. Among the Indians the land was claimed by use. The more you used, the more you possessed, the more wealth you created. And to use more and more of the land, these men brought in more white men as hired men. And these white men brought in their brothers looking for a safe refuge, a sanctuary, a no man's land where the white man's law could not touch them. These white men were quick to see the opportunities in the dark land of hills and shadows. They could rob and steal and flee to safety from the law.

In this land of five tribes and five laws, with still another law for the white men far away in Fort Smith, it was the old friend, the clan that could be trusted. These trusted ones remembered the old ways. In the old ways, a man did not steal or lie. In the old ways, the taking of blood required the taking of blood. There were no degrees of guilt, no manslaughter or accidental homicide. A man who took a life must give his life. He must walk up to the victim's family or the tribal Light Horse police and give himself up to be taken to the place of execution. There a heart was pinned to his chest, and he was shot with arrow or bullet. The old sense of honor, of disgrace strengthened the bond with the close friend and the clan in this land of shifting shadows and desperadoes.

In the 1870s many in the Nations still remembered the long trip west and the burden on their souls caused by the betrayal of the white men and their own white blood. A new generation of young men who had fought in the War between the States, either as Union or Confederate, carried a new burden of defeat as ex-Rebels denigrated by Reconstruction or as ex-soldiers forgotten again by their country. It was easy to gather such men against any enemy from without. The railroad became a symbol to them of the long betrayal.

John Skinny wrote the message out, then sat looking at it.

Mr. Ira Wolf,
My brother has been detained. Please make the necessary arrangements with the railroad at Three Forks.
Boudinot

To a casual reader, a white man, the message seemed innocuous, no cause for alarm, but Indian eyes would read it differently.

Skinny got up quickly, holding the flimsy paper, and headed up the wide, deeply rutted street to the Three Forks Hotel and Store. The hotel consisted of three side-railed railroad cars, and the store was the fourth. According to the law, it only sold alcohol to white men, never Indians. The boy went inside and leaned over the plank bar set on kegs to talk to the keeper who served as trader to the rest of the community.

"What is it, John?" the fat man wrapped in an apron asked the boy telegrapher.

"Message for Ira Wolf," Skinny replied.

"He's playin' cards in the last car. All of 'em are out there." The trader seemed to rub his words into the top of the bar.

John Skinny descended the steps of the saloon-store car and headed back along the tracks. He listened for voices as he moved beside the sleeping cars. He heard only a rumble of heavy snores. One man sat with his head in his hands on the back steps, but the boy did not look too closely at him. From a quick side glance, Skinny judged this man had already had a hard night. Any lip or perceived insult could bring him off the iron steps like lightning, the big pistol he wore at his hip in his shaking hand. John Skinny caught the handrail and swung up onto the steps of the last car. He knocked on the door. The drunk on the adjoining platform closed his eyes and moaned.

163

"Just go on in, kid. This ain't formal," he whispered hoarsely. The boy rapped on the door again, rattling the etched glass. The drunk's burning eyes shot toward him as he reached for his gun. "By God, kid, you deaf? Go on in."

Skinny swallowed and opened the door. He eased through, keeping very close to the exit, but out of reach of the man outside. Before him lay the long interior of the car, stripped bare of seats, and furnished, instead, with tables, chairs, and a few bunks. It was a place of depths and shadows except for the circle of light at the far end. Ira Wolf and several other men were playing cards.

They were dark men. They wore their straight black hair long or in tight braids that fell over calico or denim shirts. The hair of the 'breeds was lighter and curled into brown cowlicks at the back of their heads. One of the men had a new barbershop haircut that made him look skinned and awkward and showed he had been in a white man's jail.

"What do you want?" growled a man, sitting next to the door with a shotgun cradled in his arms.

The boy waved the flimsy paper. "I have a message for Mister Wolf from Mister Boudinot."

The man stood up and took the telegram from the boy. "Well, what the hell you waiting for?" he asked.

"Not a thing." The boy swallowed his words and started to duck out.

"Aw, come on!" The door tender shifted his gun, caught the boy's arm, and shoved him forward toward the circle of light. "The cap'n may want to talk to you."

Pushing the boy in front of him, the man with the shotgun walked heavily down to the card game and laid the telegram on the table in front of Ira Wolf. Wolf pushed the paper into the light. As he read it, he laid his cards face up on the table.

"Game's over, fellas. Watie Boudinot has been arrested. Eli don't want the train to go past this stop. Possum, you get the boys from out at Shag Hollow. Bill, we'll need Simon Little Elk's kin. Nate, see who you can dig up down along the river. Make sure they're sober or can be by the time the train gets here. They may have to use their guns. Just be ready."

The group of 'bloods and 'breeds scooted back their chairs, noisily, over the hollow-sounding floor. They picked up guns and hats near the door and walked out in white men's brogans or boots to get the help Boudinot would need. Nate Johnson paused at the door, holding the frame as he turned back into the room. "You think there's goin' to be any killin'?"

Ira Wolf looked up from the table into the outlaw's eyes. "Could be. Boudinot is crazy over that worthless kid."

Johnson rubbed his chin with a rough hand. "Watie ain't even shit," he murmured as he went out into the night.

Ira Wolf meditated on those words for a moment. He pulled a revolver from his waist and laid it on the table in front of him near the abandoned stakes. Slowly he spread his copper hands and placed them on the table. John Skinny's nose suddenly itched like it had never itched, and he shuffled as he rubbed it. Wolf looked up at the slight noise. His hand slid over the weapon.

"Thanks, kid." Wolf slipped the gun back into his belt. "Tonight you ain't workin' for the railroad. You're workin' for us." And the boy knew that "us" meant more than Boudinot and Wolf and the men at the table. "You sit on that wire. Nothing going out from here or coming in that I don't see and approve. Boudinot will want to send a message, when he gets in. Be ready. I don't want to hunt for you." His black eyes studied the young mixed-blood in front of him. "You got that?" The boy nodded. Wolf tossed Skinny a five-dollar gold piece from the pile of money on the table. The youth caught it with both hands. "Get down there to your key where you can be of use."

The Prairie Queen sped on through the night while her privileged passengers slept or sat

166

looking into the blackness. Moving now as an express without the immigrant cars she had dropped at McAlester, she would stop only when water was necessary. The train would be in St. Louis ahead of schedule. The miles disappeared in monotonous clicks as she moved over the rail joints, length by length, deeper into the darkness of the Nations.

Just before midnight, the engine whistled two short bursts and braked into the Three Forks Station. All appeared normal. The water tower chute was lowered. The water flowed by gravity into the engine's thirsty throat, filling the empty belly. Steam hissed and rose into the night as the cold water hit the hot metal. Preoccupied with their chores, the crew did not see the armed men who silently walked out of the shadows and stole their train.

"Get dressed, folks," the steward called out shakily as he proceeded through the car with a pistol snugged against his back. "Come on, folks, now. Get dressed. Get yourselves out onto the platform." He tapped doors as he passed. "Yes, sir, move yourselves right out of here. Come on, folks. You got time to get dressed, but don't dally now."

Mari sat up as the porter and his escort passed. She quickly lifted the shade for a fleeting look out into the night. There were men with guns

167

along the side of the train. As she dressed, there was a small knock at the door. She slid it open, stepping into her riding skirt. It was Susan Marn.

"Father wants to know what's going on. What you see."

"I'm not sure," replied Mari in a low voice. She glanced at the big man with a shotgun in his arms at the rear door. "Tell him there are armed men on and around the train. It looks like the train has been taken."

"What kind of men?"

"They seem to be mostly Indians, probably decent enough . . . not thugs."

The gunmen made sure that all the passengers funneled down the aisles and out the door nearest the station. Any attempt at altering the route was quickly turned back by the stern face of a man with his hand resting casually on a gun. Disembarking, the travelers looked about the darkness. Here and there the windows or lanterns of the rough town created pools of light against the black shadows. A soft rain had started. By morning the street would be six inches of red mud or a river depending on the volume of the downpour.

During the slow, short parade to the station, Mari caught sight of the train crew lying on their bellies, tied hand and foot at the base of the water tower. Leaning against its iron legs, against the walls of the station, against wagons parked about the yard, grim-faced citizens of the Nations lightly balanced heavy rifles against their elbows or rested their callused hands on the butts of Army pistols. They watched silently. Their faces revealed nothing, not hate or greed or fear. Mari had seen the unreadable masks before, among the Apaches. As they neared the door, the car steward was taken away to join the rest of the crew.

"Are you going to leave those men tied up in the rain?" Mari asked a man beside the door. He did not respond, but pushed her inside.

Standing under the porch, Ira Wolf studied the men wallowing in the increasing downpour. He walked out into the slush, water streaming from his hat, and yelled at his men. They dragged the crew beneath the water tower.

Inside Mrs. Todd fumed. "What is going on now? People can't be jerked about like this in the middle of the night."

"I bet it's got something to do with that 'breed they took off the train," offered Joe Crites.

Mrs. Todd glared at the man's continuing insistence upon betting on anything and everything.

"That's it!" exclaimed Beecher. "We've been taken hostage for that bandit."

"All of us?" Mari asked quietly as she looked over her companions in the station.

A thought formed in Crites's speculating mind. "Holding all of us would start a war. Rile the whole country. Wouldn't be tolerated. But what about one of us . . . one who's important to the railroad. One of us is bound to be a valuable commodity." Crites paused, assessing the situation. "I'd give odds on that. I mean, I've traveled in some nice cars, but I never seen one as nice as the arrangements on *The Prairie Queen*. Never had a special dining car or stewards crawling all over me. Never cut loose the rest of the train to make time, either. Somebody important is aboard this train, and somebody somewhere is in a hurry to see them."

Captain Howard rested comfortably against a post in the unpainted station room. From the shadows he noticed that the lantern behind Mari made a halo of her hair, softly shadowed the high cheek bones as she worked the tension from her neck and shoulders with her hands. Her hair was short now. He remembered it as being long. She must have a heavy hairpiece, he thought, that she attaches when she is in public. In her hurry to leave the car, she had not bothered with the ornament. He noticed that the short hair curled softly along her jaw. As usual, he thought, Mari had done what was practical and convenient with little regard for convention. She was dressed simply, flat boots, a riding skirt, a white shirt beneath a short jacket.

170

He walked forward until he was standing behind her. "Why'd you cut your hair?"

She turned to him without uncrossing her arms. "I was broke and needed a stake for a poker game. The only thing I had left to sell was my hair. I bought it back later. But by then I'd gotten to like the freedom of not having it."

"You always liked to be free," Howard said, remembering. "Nothing you wouldn't do for your freedom."

Mari looked at him closely. "My freedom *is* important to me, Doc. That's why I'd never give it up without a lot of thought."

"You!" A surly 'breed pointed at Mrs. Omar Todd from the upstairs landing of the dépôt stairs. "Up here!" One of the guards pushed the sagging little woman toward the crude stairway.

"Courage, Missus Todd," called out Mari.

Mrs. Todd shrugged off the guard's hand and straightened imperiously.

As Mrs. Todd climbed slowly up toward the Indian, Joe Crites eased in beside Beecher and put his hand against the post. "Wonder what happened to Boudinot? I thought he was right behind me. You suppose he got in trouble with some of these rascals?"

"I doubt it. They probably just detained him in the car to question him," suggested Beecher.

"I don't know." Crites looked about furtively. "He is an Indian."

"I haven't seen the passenger in Compartment One either," said Beecher.

"Hey, that guy is invisible." Crites's words were light, but not his voice or his eyes.

Chapter Fourteen

Eli Boudinot sat comfortably at a table bathed in light as Mrs. Todd entered. "Please sit down, Missus Todd," he spoke softly. But he did not rise to pull out her chair. She considered the lack of proper deference. Then, as though Boudinot and the guard were beneath her contempt, she drew out the chair herself and sat.

Boudinot, the gentleman traveler, had changed. The white man's suit was gone. He wore, instead, a fringed leather jacket over his white shirt. His pants were now stuffed into tall riding boots.

"What business do you have in Saint Louis?" he asked the woman without preliminaries.

"I live there. That's all," Mrs. Todd replied.

"What is your source of income?"

"That is not your business, sir."

Boudinot's eyes narrowed. He did not raise his voice, but Mrs. Todd did not doubt his command of the situation. "I have made it my business. Answer my question."

"My deceased husband left me well cared for, if I'm careful," the little woman said guardedly.

"You can afford to travel? This coach wasn't cheap, Missus Todd. Why were you in Texas?" continued the Indian.

"My son works for the railroad. I went to visit

him," she blustered. "He provided the tickets. I don't pay a cent, if it's any of your business."

"Oh, it is my business, I assure you. And what does your son do for the railroad?" pursued Boudinot.

"He's a track engineer," Mrs. Todd said. "Learned it in the late war."

"He arranged your first-class passage?" asked Boudinot.

"That's right. That's what I said. They think a lot of him at the railroad," Mrs. Todd answered proudly, a few centimeters taller in her chair.

Boudinot studied her with blue eyes half concealed by heavy lids. After long moments his attention turned to his fingers spread out on the table top. "You can go," he directed.

Mrs. Todd descended with a flutter. "It's Mister Boudinot," she began explaining to the others below, once she was halfway down the flight of stairs. "Upstairs. Dressed up like an Indian. He wants you next, Mister Crites."

Crites straightened, irritably rocking slightly, moving his shoulders from side to side. "Thank you, Missus Todd, for that information." He moved off, muttering to himself. "I just had to say there wasn't any future in being an Indian. *It's a white man's world* . . . I said that."

One of the guards brushed casually against Susan Marn, watching her reaction, assessing the capabilities of the old mountain man. Josh Marn sensed something, but was unsure how to counter.

Mari's eyes watched the scene closely. She rose and crossed to sit on the oak bench, unobtrusively putting herself between the girl and the guard.

"Thank you, Mari," old Marn whispered.

By the time Joe Crites returned, the passengers had shifted groups and positions in the room, but all knew Boudinot was upstairs conducting the interrogations. Their eyes were on Crites as he descended the dimly lit stairway.

"Well?" Mrs. Todd turned to Crites. "What'd he want?" The others were also listening.

"Wanted to know if I had some special business, I guess. I think he's looking for a hostage to trade for that 'breed that was taken away. He's pretty sure that there is someone on board who's seriously important to the railroad."

"What's that got to do with anything?" asked Mrs. Todd.

"It all revolves around this. The man they took off the train in McAlester robbed a train. My guess is that Boudinot thinks he can find somebody among us to trade to the railroad for him. Once he's got a bargaining chip, the rest of us can go on . . . probably. That's what I think he's figuring on." Crites was now the gambler calculating the odds. "Maybe."

"Surely the whole bunch of us would be worth

more than just one person," said Mrs. Todd, looking at the other passengers.

"That's not the way Boudinot wants to handle it, I'd bet," Crites thought aloud. "If I can figure out one hostage is better than the lot, so can he. I don't think he's an unreasonable man. I think he'd like to do things as easy as possible. That's what I think."

"Well, you shared a compartment," observed Beecher. "You know him better than any of us."

As speculation on Boudinot's plan circulated among the passengers, they began to wonder who among them could free the rest.

"Well, I hope he finds his hostage quickly," Beecher said. "Right, Howard?"

"Quick or slow, it's inevitable." Phillip Howard blew a smoke ring into the air. "But why make it easy on that savage?"

Upstairs, Boudinot sat looking at the table top, sorting the information he had from his men, and the two passengers he had talked with, deciding to release all for one, if he could find the right one. He stood and walked around the table to the door.

Entering the upstairs hall, Boudinot leaned on the banister that ran around it. "I have decided not to detain all of you. I will only keep one of you to exchange. One of you is extremely important to the railroad. You know who you are. If you will step forward, your fellow passengers can go on their way now without further delay." Boudinot looked down on the people gathered in the waiting room below. As his eyes moved over them, the eyes of the passengers turned away. "Very well, then, if there is no volunteer, I will continue my search. The priest . . . Reyneau. Miss Marshay, I will need a translator. Please come up with Reyneau."

Once upstairs, Father Reyneau sat down at the table and placed his hands palms down on its surface. Mari slipped into the chair beside him.

"We found this in your papers, priest." Boudinot tossed a loose sheet on the table. Mari saw the color drain from the Frenchman's face. He did not reach for the folded letter, but, instead, drew his hands back as if from a stinging poisonous insect. "What does this mean?"

Mari translated and waited for the Frenchman's reply. "It means he was removed from his position. He was defrocked for . . ."—she listened as Reyneau continued to explain—"for matters too embarrassing to discuss."

Boudinot considered the thought. "Too embarrassing. Thief? Drunkard? Womanizer? Homosexual? Pedophile? Hum. Why, then, do you wear this costume?"

Mari again put the question to Reyneau and waited for the response. "He was visiting his family in New Orleans. Now he is going to visit

177

his sister in Saint Louis, and he does not want her to know of his disgrace. She would worry, and she is not well."

"Stand up, priest, and take off your clothes," Boudinot ordered quietly.

Mari looked at the half-breed, trying to read his face, seeing it differently from the afternoon and the evening at dinner. "You can't . . . ," she began.

"You will not be embarrassed, Miss Marshay. I assure you it won't come to that."

"It's not that. It's not right to ask this of . . . of anyone," protested Mari.

"Tell him to undress."

Even as Mari translated, the former priest began to disrobe. He slowly unbuttoned the black cassock. Boudinot's eyes watched him closely. "This priest, Miss Marshay, whom you, The Pagan, would protect, was attached to the Vatican. He was a secretary to one of its financial administrators. He is an embezzler. No records and no money were recovered. Ah!" Boudinot rose quickly to his feet and snatched the buckle on the money belt strapped around the man's waist. "Money does not evaporate, does it, priest? It goes somewhere, and someone can eventually go and get it." Boudinot roughly jerked the belt loose and tossed it on the floor. "I absolve you of your guilt. From now on it's mine." The lawyer sat heavily in his chair and brushed back the hair that had fallen across his face. "You can go." A civilized man again, Boudinot handed Reyneau his papers. The Frenchman bowed slightly. Mari rose from her chair to leave with the priest, following him toward the door as he readjusted his habiliment.

Boudinot's voice stopped the woman. "Please remain, Miss Marshay."

Returning to the table, Mari stood outside the circle of light that surrounded Boudinot. Reyneau hesitated at the door, then, alone, went down to the others.

"Do you have an important friend in Saint Louis, Miss Marshay?" queried the Indian.

"I have no friends." Mari moved away from the table, prowling restlessly in the shadows.

"Your family is important, willing to pay for your safe return?"

"My family is gone. What remain have forgotten me," she answered. The woman continued her circuit around the room.

"Why are you going to Saint Louis?" Boudinot asked, following her with his eyes.

"To buy a new hat." Mari indolently pushed back a wall of mosquito netting that divided the table and chairs from the galley area with its stove and stack of dirty dishes.

"Where do you stay in Saint Louis?"

"At the Saint Charles," the woman replied.

"That's an expensive hotel," observed Boudinot. Mari smiled, but said nothing. "Do you

179

make the trip between New Orleans and Saint Louis often?"

"Every three or four months. Sometimes more often, sometimes less," Mari said.

"Why?"

"They are interesting cities," the woman said.

"Is this trunk yours?" asked Boudinot, setting the small leather trunk on the table.

Mari glanced at it and sighed. "It's mine."

"And it's contents?"

"Mine."

"No embezzling?"

"No embezzling."

"No cheating at cards?" She shook her head. "It's a lot of money, Miss Marshay." Boudinot opened the trunk. The lock had been broken. "I'm afraid my friends damaged the lock in their haste." Boudinot began to lay out the bundles of money on the table top. Mari watched. "All U.S. money. Win it all in one game? That's high stakes."

"It has taken me three years to accumulate that," she said softly, watching the Indian's continued shuffling of the bundles. "It's a hundred and fifty thousand dollars. You don't have to count it."

"I'm not counting it. I'm just trying to see what is at the bottom of this pile of money." The woman looked away while drumming her fingers on the stove. Boudinot placed a sheaf of papers

180

on the table after glancing at them. "Had you rather I not see the picture of Doctor Howard?"

"There is also a picture of my father, a miniature of my mother, and some other pictures," she noted.

"All treasures to be sure. Ah, a little boy . . . handsome. Family?"

"My godson."

"His name?"

"Richard."

"Well, there are no other men's pictures I see, just Howard. Very valuable, I suppose."

"I'd forgotten I had it."

Boudinot studied her face for the lie if it were there. "You will wait here, in the sleeping room."

"You've made a pretty good haul this evening, Mister Boudinot. I really did not expect you to be a thief."

"Thief? Is that what you think I am? I'm not a thief, Miss Marshay. Tonight I'm a simple merchant. Tonight I have something I wish to purchase, so I am looking at the inventory available to me for something . . . or someone . . . to exchange for it."

"It's not your money, Mister Boudinot. It's mine."

"The money is important to you?"

"It is."

"To buy new hats and dresses, a house, a carriage?"

"To buy my independence," Mari said.

"From whom?"

"That, sir, is not your business."

"Very well . . . for now. I will think about it. What about the priest's money? Would that help you?"

"It is not mine, Mister Boudinot."

"I offer it freely."

"It isn't yours, either."

"You are surely correct, Miss Marshay. But I have custody of it and of yours, also. So much money. Three years." He thought a moment. "I do not think you are a gambler, at all. From my experience I've never met a gambler who could quit while he had a coin in his pocket. This money, not the game, is important to you. But, I wonder, would you risk it all in the right situation?"

Boudinot took Mari's elbow and directed her past the stove, through the masses of mosquito netting into the dingy sleeping room. He closed the louvered door behind her. Mari sighed at the shabby room. A door beyond the stacked beds opened onto the landing that overlooked the gathering room below. She climbed onto the still unmade upper bunk and drew her legs up. Wrapping her arms around them, she rested her chin on her knees.

The interrogations continued in the next room as, one by one, the other passengers and members of the train crew were brought before Boudinot. Unable to bear the idleness, Mari made the unmade beds in the sleeping room and straightened the clutter. She picked up a dirty plate and cup and stepped to the hall door. A young Indian man stood outside.

"Please go and get me a couple of buckets of clean water," she said to the startled youth.

Mari walked through the sleeping room to the small galley kitchen with the dirty plate and cup. Scraping the pieces of foods into a slop can, she began to sort the pots and dishes. Boudinot turned to see what the woman was doing, but he did not send her back to the sleeping room. He returned to his questioning of John Beecher. The preacher's eyes followed her about her work. Taking no notice of the men or the questioning, Mari shook the teakettle, opened it to see how much water was inside, then set it on the stove to heat. She removed her jacket and hung it on a hook. She stripped a feed sack towel from a hook and wrapped it around her waist as a makeshift apron. She unbuttoned her cuffs and rolled up the sleeves of her immaculate white shirt as the guard entered with the water. He passed Beecher, leaving the room, at the door. Boudinot grimaced slightly as he observed the young 'breed with his rifle pinched under his arm and a bucketful of water in each hand. Mari smiled at the boy and handed him the box of tin cans and trash to empty. Boudinot's eyes followed the self-conscious youth.

"I want to see the conductor and engineer again," he said as the young man went to the door. "Put down that trash." The boy stooped to set it down. "Not here!" Boudinot began to pace as he waited for his next interview. He glanced at Mari, but she was absorbed in the work at hand.

She poured the contents of one bucket into a large metal pan, cut some slivers from a cake of lye soap, and added the hot water from the teakettle. Refilling the kettle from one of the buckets, she put it back on the fire to boil. She whirled the dishwater with a wooden spoon, dissolving the soap. Then she began to wash the dishes. As she washed, she piled them all into a second pan. When it was full and the kettle again boiling, she poured the steaming water over them before draining them on another towel beside the basins. She ignored Boudinot. His brow knit, but he said nothing as he watched.

Ira Wolf and another Indian entered.

"More papers from the passengers," Wolf noted as he placed a stack of documents before his leader.

Boudinot shuffled through the pile, perusing the information set before him. Wolf and his partner watched the progress of the woman's work. Boudinot read. He barely flinched when a pot slid off the counter and crashed to the floor. Mari smiled apologetically and began to dry the dishes and set them into a cupboard. She found a broom and brushed up the grit and gravel from the board floor and collected it into a pan. When she looked up, Boudinot was standing above her, hands on his hips. She slowly straightened with the dustpan in her hand.

"Miss Marshay, I do not want you out of that room again," Boudinot said sharply, pointing at the sleeping room. "Stay in the room where I put you until I ask you to come out. And do not talk to the guards or ask them to do any further services."

She handed him the pan and broom. "Fine," she said, and returned to the sleeping room, closing the louvered door behind her.

The door immediately popped back open. She walked to a cup left on the dry sink, dumped a spoonful of tea into it, and poured boiling water from the stove over it. She shrugged slightly at Boudinot as she retrieved her jacket.

"Miss Marshay." Boudinot frowned.

"I'll be very comfortable now, thank you. Don't bother yourself about me. There's sugar in here," she said, returning to the open door of the smaller room.

Boudinot caught her arm. He held her for a moment. His voice was civil and calm, but his words carried an intensity that made her certain of the man's intent. "Do not come out of that room again unless you are called. This is a dangerous place at a dangerous moment. I would not risk your life, but it may be that I cannot protect it if you are reckless, Miss Marshay. Do you understand?" As her eyes ran over his face, she nodded. Boudinot bowed slightly as she went into the small room. He pulled the door shut sharply.

Chapter Fifteen

Mari sipped the tea as she looked over the still dismal room. At last she set down the cup and climbed onto a bunk. She rested with her jacket across her eyes. In the next room she could hear the soft voices of the Indians as they moved about and discussed their plans. She struggled with the words. For a long time, the sounds were not clear or in a tongue she could understand. Then she heard Boudinot say distinctly: "Yes. This is it. Bring him up."

Hearing the sound of the door opening and closing and the hurried footsteps down the hall and stairway, Mari wondered what the words had meant: *This is it.* Perhaps Boudinot had found his hostage. He had remained behind in the room. She felt his restless presence in the room beyond the door, pacing back and forth between the window and table. Finally he sat down heavily. Smoke from his cigar drifted through the air. Mari waited, listening.

"Sit down, Doctor Howard," Boudinot's voice finally came from the next room. Mari removed the jacket from her face and sat up. Quietly she dropped from the bunk and moved toward the door that separated her from the interrogation room. Although she could not see Phillip Howard, she listened intently through the louvered door.

"I prefer to stand," the physician said, declining his captor's hospitality.

"As you choose," Boudinot said. "I'm sure you know by now that I'm looking for a hostage of significant value to exchange for my brother."

Howard nodded.

"Why are you going to Saint Louis, Doctor?" Boudinot asked, dropping onto the lighted table a sheaf of Howard's personal papers brought from the train.

"I have an operation to perform," Howard answered.

Boudinot drew out a telegram. "Who is your patient?" Howard observed the telegram, but said nothing. Boudinot looked up. "Is your patient Richard Huxley?"

"That's correct."

"What is paraplegia?" asked Boudinot.

"It's a paralysis of the lower limbs caused, in this instance, by pressure on the spinal nerves from a bullet," responded the doctor. "A shooting accident."

"And you are the only man who is able to do the surgery that will relieve the pressure?"

Howard nodded.

"Thank you, Doctor Howard!" Boudinot raked the papers before him into a neat pile and offered them back to Phillip Howard. Smiling, he tossed the telegram on top. "You have given me my hostage. Alfred Huxley will not hesitate to hasten the release of my brother to save his son. And no one will argue with the head of the railroad and a personal friend of the President of the United States. You will wait here while I see that a message is sent at once. You see, the longer I hold this station, the greater the risk of fighting a small war. Even now we teeter on the brink. We still have the element of surprise in our favor. But if someone decides to take the situation into his own hands. . . . It is a delicate balance. We are desperate men, lost men, Doctor Howard."

"Bit meler-dramatic," Howard observed casually, almost contemptuously. "Good Lord, Boudinot, you're a lawyer. Why don't you just go through the courts . . . do things correctly? Avoid all these theatrics and inconvenience to everyone?"

"I am a lawyer." Boudinot tipped back in the chair. "I know the system well enough to use it at any rate. But my little brother is an Indian. He'll die in a jail cell."

"Perhaps you don't give him credit," the doctor pursued. "He may well be made of sterner stuff than you believe. Toughen up and come through it a better man, all that."

"You are familiar with the trial of the Kiowa chiefs at Jacksboro . . . Satanta and Big Tree?" asked Boudinot.

"I've heard about it. Actually read Doctor

Patzki's report. The Kiowas butchered a group of teamsters who were hauling corn. Hung one of the men upside down over a fire, cut out his tongue. Mutilated them all."

"You are well informed on the medical details," concluded Boudinot. "And do you doubt that the chiefs were guilty?"

"Not one bit," the captain spoke squarely.

"My brother is guilty, also, Doctor Howard. He would also surely be convicted of robbing the Katy Railroad at Limestone Gap."

Boudinot stood, shoved the chair under the table, and placed his hands carefully on its back. "Two of the Kiowa chiefs, Satanta and Big Tree, rode the first Katy into Texas on Christmas night. Old Satank had already eaten away his own flesh to get the cuffs off and committed suicide by getting the young guards to shoot him. My brother followed the trial . . . the suicide . . . very closely. He vowed that he would kill himself if he were ever put in prison. He cannot bear the thought of confinement, even temporary confinement. For him it's like being put alive in a coffin.

"My brother is a drunk, a whoremonger, and a train robber, but he is not a killer. Sending him through the system, first through a trial and then jail, would be, in effect, sentencing him to death for a non-capital crime. I won't permit that. You see, Doctor, I must work differently here. It's a

190

matter between him and the railroad. No one was harmed. And, now, I have something dear to the owner of the railroad, Mister Alfred Huxley. It is his son's life against my brother's. We can talk on common terms. I believe he will drop the charges and have my brother returned. We will know when I have sent my telegram. Show Doctor Howard to the secure room," Boudinot ordered one of his men. "You will wait there, sir. I believe you will be comfortable."

Mari heard the men's heavy boots on the floorboards, heard them descend the stairs. The upstairs tier of rooms was suddenly very quiet. The shadow of one of the guards moved across the louvered door. She heard his soft breathing and stepped back from the door.

St. Louis, Missouri

Anne Mary Huxley awakened her husband, Commodore H. Albert Huxley, shortly after midnight. An urgent telegram had been delivered. He sat up in bed and read the words by the light of the lamp his wife had lit for him.

"My God," he whispered. "A man named Eli Boudinot has Doctor Howard. He wants to exchange him for his brother, Watie. We've apparently charged him with robbing the train at Limestone Gap. Marshals have taken him into custody at McAlester. This Eli Boudinot wants all the charges dropped." Huxley studied the paper as he thought.

"Can you do that, Alfred?" Anne Mary asked gently.

Huxley's eyes popped with fire. "I can do anything I damn' well please. I'm president of the Missouri, Kansas, and Texas Railroad. Is the messenger waiting for a reply, Anne Mary?"

Anne Mary Huxley nodded. Her husband sat on the side of the bed with his head in his hands. "Have him come up. Then send someone for Steve Taylor. I want all charges dropped against Watie Boudinot, and then I want him sent to Three Forks Station by the fastest possible train." As his wife turned to leave, her husband asked softly: "How's Richard?"

Tears swam up over the lids of the woman's eyes. The child had come to her late, the long-sought fulfillment in a world of material riches. "He's so small, so brave," she said. "He doesn't fight the straps and packing, at all. He's lying there like the perfect soldier, waiting for his doctor to come. Oh, Albert, the doctor must do something soon. Richard's just a little boy . . . not a soldier. We shouldn't have given him that gun."

Huxley crossed the carpet to his wife. "It was an accident, Anne Mary. He can't live in a prison of our overprotection. He has a right to be a child like other children. It was just a horrible accident." He held her in his arms. "I'll come in and sit with you when I'm sure everything is moving along, my dear. I'll read to him of heroes when he wakes up. Doctor Howard will arrive as fast as my train can get him here, even if I have to wire the President. I won't put up with any delays. I'll wire the President now." He said the last words almost to himself, then looked down at his wife. "Someday when Richard is walking and running again, we'll think how foolish we were to worry so much."

"Mari is on that train, too, Alfred. She was coming to be with us."

"Don't worry." Huxley drew his wife to him, lifting her face to his own. "Mari is a smart woman. The brigand may not know who she is. He seems intent on exchanging his brother for Howard." He patted her comfortingly as he held her. "Simeon Kraul is also on that train. Pity him, if they find out." Huxley held his wife very close, vowing: "As it is in my power, the doctor will be here as quickly as possible. As it is in my power, I will kill any man who interferes."

Chapter Sixteen

Three Forks Station, Indian Territory

After sending the telegram with his offer to H. Alfred Huxley, Boudinot sat in the upstairs room drinking a cup of coffee he had made for himself. The room was quiet, the man pensive. For the first time since Watie had been taken, Boudinot felt confident that events were proceeding on the right course. So far, he had successfully skated along the edge of disaster. No one would be hurt or seriously delayed. He had made the situation a matter between Huxley and himself. Watie would be out of the hands of the law, his crime wiped away. He was young, and surely he had learned something from this scare. Boudinot walked to the window and stood, hands behind his back. Pondering the rain, he slowly crossed his fingers. He would need luck, but it could work—no one hurt, no one killed, a simple exchange—unless, of course, something happened to the Huxley boy, a child.

As the exterior door of the interrogation room burst open, Boudinot turned. Ira Wolf spoke fiercely. "Look what we found, Eli!"

In her bunk, Mari heard the suppressed anger in Wolf's voice. The skin on her neck and forearms rose in tiny bumps of foreboding upon the entry of a new and more sinister presence into the situation at Three Forks.

"Locked up tighter than a tin drum," Wolf said beyond the door.

Wolf pointed with a heavy-bladed shingle hatchet as two large Indians dragged a man across the floor toward Boudinot. They dumped him into the chair in the circle of light. "Says he's Pierpoint Cable, but we found these papers on him." He walked over to Boudinot and handed him several folded sheets of paper.

"Get your hands off me, you filthy red niggers!" the new arrival hissed.

Boudinot glanced at the papers as Wolf pointed, then stood silently in the shadows, closely watching the man.

"What the hell do you want from me?" the prisoner shouted. He strained to see Boudinot in the darkness. "I'm an invalid. I can't be thrown about like this." The pale man pushed back the wisps of thin hair that fell in disarray across his forehead. "I need my hat . . . there's a draft in here."

"You are lucky to still be alive," Boudinot's voice came from across the room.

"You can't threaten me like some commercial traveler. I am a man of a certain influence," the invalid said, as the two Indians who had pushed him into the chair in front of the table stationed themselves several steps back.

195

"Shut up and listen very carefully. These men aren't fools. And neither am I. We are going to examine the value of that certain influence. Shall we begin?" Boudinot walked to the table, sat down silently, and began an examination of the papers that had been set on the table. Both the diligence and the experience of his legal training showed in his concentration.

The invalid took in the room around him as Boudinot read. His eyes came to rest on the money lying on the table. His glove-wrapped fingers twitched involuntarily.

Boudinot saw the convulsive movement. "Would you like to have two hundred thousand dollars tonight?"

Pierpoint Cable smiled. "Perhaps there is some service I can perform."

"My need is very simple. I want my brother back here before morning. I want it done quietly between those involved . . . myself, my brother, and the Katy Railroad . . . without any gun play."

"Where is he now?"

"He's in the jail in McAlester."

"What did he do?" asked Cable suspiciously, concerned about the amount of work involved, not the legality. "Murder is hard to gloss over."

"He just robbed a train . . . did a few hundred dollars' damage."

Cable's forehead wrinkled. He began unobtrusively, like a snake edging toward a chick, to assume control. "Train robbery is serious. How much was taken? Will there be restitution? How much? Two hundred thousand?" Cable's gloved hand covered one of the stacks of bills. His thumb fondled it. "That may not be enough." His fingers closed tightly as his hand jerked away from the money.

Boudinot watched the brightness of the invalid's eyes, his growing energy, his shift from victim to manipulator, controller.

It was the eyes that made him certain he had dealt with the man before. This man was leaner, gaunt, compared to his former corpulent self. Boudinot had heard he was given to strange health regimes. The thick muttonchop whiskers and beard were gone. There was an overall monkish appearance to the man now. His physical appearance had undergone a tremendous change, but the eyes still glittered with the deep-burning fire of greed and self-interest. This traveler was no invalid, no victim of poor health. His transformation was the metamorphosis of a shriveled soul.

As Boudinot recalled, it was raining then, also, the first time he had heard the name Simeon Kraul. The tribal men had gathered to confer about the railroad crossing their land. They were angry. But they were not the primitive figures depicted in newspapers and sentimental novels. They were men long educated by contact with the ways and methods of the white man. They would not attack their enemy with bows and arrows or even rifles. They would use the tools the whites had shown them—influence, legislation. Once before they had relied on the law, had taken their case over the Eastern homelands to the highest court and won there. Ultimately they lost when those with personal influence and power persuaded President Andrew Jackson not to enforce their victory. With the railroad hungering for their new lands, they had sought to develop their own influence—Simeon Kraul had been the key. He had made it known that a few important men in Washington were willing to consider the red men's cause. Naturally, he had casually noted, if these men were not reëlected, they could not vote nor would they have any influence in the future of the railroad. Kraul had made it plain—it took money to get elected, to buy votes.

"It's more than enough, Cable, or should I say . . . Kraul," Boudinot said softly. Kraul seemed startled but quickly recovered himself. "Yes," Boudinot continued, "we know you are Simeon Kraul. We have dealt with you before. Perhaps you are a bit puzzled about that past meeting. But, then, you have cheated so many it must be hard to remember. All that is necessary is that you remember this. You will not be receiving any money this time. I won't make the mistake of trusting you and giving you money again. This is not my money. I can't offer it to you. But if it were, I still would not. We've been down this road before. You are the man we sent Pleasant Carter to see in Washington. You are the man Pleasant Carter gave all the money that we could raise to help a certain politician's campaign. We sold our ponies and our sheep and cattle. We took the food from our children's mouths. We expected some relief on the railroad votes, Kraul. Later, when our man met with your man, the candidate we financed, he didn't know, couldn't remember who we were. As I recall, he said we'd have to give him more money, and, then, he'd see what he could do to protect our land. But, of course, we had no more money. We had already given you everything. You robbed us, Kraul, as surely as my brother robbed the Katy Railroad." Boudinot paused briefly.

"Money is so important, isn't it, Kraul? Well, tonight it is worthless. The currency is your life for my brother." Boudinot's eyes narrowed to blue slits. "You are going to have to call in your chips, Kraul, your favors. You're going to have to use every secret you know about anybody and everybody to get my brother here by morning . . . or I will kill you." There was no drama, no bravado in Boudinot's words. He spoke quietly as a man who had killed and who would kill again if necessary.

Kraul sat for a minute analyzing Boudinot's

words and the situation. He licked his teeth. He considered Ira Wolf, palming the hatchet. "You wouldn't dare kill me, Boudinot." He paused. "I think money would get the job done . . . get what you want."

"I've told you I won't give you any money this time." Boudinot placed the stack of bills back in the small trunk and closed the lid. He dropped the money belt on top. "Return this to Miss Marshay's compartment," he said to one of his men standing near Kraul. "You are a long way from civilization here, Kraul, a long way from your influential friends. Your power is wasted on us, sir. *We* are the power here. And we have nothing to lose. You will simply disappear into the Nations. Nothing will ever be found. Remember, you were never actually seen by any of the passengers on the train. If questioned, they couldn't say for sure you got on or got off. You've been known to slip away before."

Kraul sat thinking. The faces he studied offered him nothing, not hope, not weakness, not indecision. His well-developed senses told him Boudinot and the others were capable of fulfilling the threat. "Very well. This is your game. Give me some paper. I shall send telegrams. My friends will contact their friends. I can assure you, all charges will be dropped when I am released."

Boudinot smiled. "You're a good boy tonight, Kraul."

"Don't patronize me, you red brigand bastard."
Boudinot's eyes grew very cold. He crossed his arms over his chest. "Write," he ordered as Ira Wolf placed paper and pencil before the invalid. Simeon Kraul bent to his task. He scribbled furiously. He shoved the papers across the table, one by one, to Boudinot, who read each one before placing it on the growing pile. When Kraul finished the last one, Boudinot read it, added it to the stack, which he carefully folded and placed inside his coat pocket. He smiled slightly.

"There's not one among these men who would help you," he said, patting his pocket. "They will be worried at first, perhaps they will consider helping, but then they will remember what it is that you know. They will ponder how your death will set them free. They will put down their pens and return to their warm beds peaceful for the first time in years. By their mere inaction, you will be dead. They will be free of the knowledge you possess and could use against them. Right now these telegrams are worthless. In fact, they may even endanger your life and our plan."

Boudinot turned and rested his elbows on the table and looked directly at the invalid. "So Kraul, you must write more. I want a detailed explanation of the deal you set up with Congressman Tanner concerning his involvement with my people. You will explain in detail how each of these people you've sent a message to

201

was involved. We will hang onto this confession until Watie is released, and, if he isn't, we have this confession. . . ."

"Blackmail! You can't . . . ," began Kraul.

"Ah, but I can." Boudinot sat back. "And what is more, I will, and I am. Even if I should weaken, my men won't. It was their wives and children that went without. It is their land you have been conspiring to steal."

Kraul said nothing, hesitating only briefly before he took up the pencil and began to write again. As he wrote, the Indian men watched and waited. Finally he pushed the paper across to Boudinot.

Boudinot read it twice, carefully. "This is adequate, Kraul. It unwinds a very tangled web."

"Give me the telegrams, I'll add a line." Kraul's skinny hand reached out.

Boudinot slipped the confession into his pocket. "We won't need your telegrams, Kraul. The names were all I wanted, and the confession, of course."

Kraul's face darkened with understanding. "Your brother?"

"Oh, we already have our person to exchange, Kraul. We won't need you or your cohorts. You will be able to leave as soon as the steam is built up. By the time you get to Saint Louis, a number of journalists will be waiting for you since we will have made sure they understand the extent of the corruption disclosed in this confession and your part in it. The fox left tracks tonight. Even a white man can follow these."

"You bastard!" shouted Simeon Kraul, rising to his feet. "I'll deny every word. This so-called confession was made under duress. It won't stand up in any court." Ira Wolf gently tapped the hatchet against his palm. Wise as a serpent, Kraul understood the implied threat. He gathered himself and recanted. "Very well," he wheezed. "You've won. I shall go back to my compartment now."

"You shall sit down," Boudinot said. "I'm not through with you yet. You have confessed to a crime. Councilmen of the Creek Nation have heard you. Your due punishment is next."

"You said . . . ," Kraul began with a whine that became a threat. "Watch your step. You can't punish me. You don't have the authority . . . you and your primitive Indian justice system. I'm a powerful man, with many friends. This night may not be the end of this situation . . . for you or these goons of yours."

"Shut up!" Boudinot tipped back in his chair. Then all was silent in the room, save for Simeon Kraul's wheezing breath.

Under the scrutiny of the Indians in the room, Kraul seemed to draw up into a tight ball of self-protection. Finally he spoke. "You can't do this to me. I won't fall for this . . . this silent treatment. You've gotten all you'll ever get out of me. Don't expect my help once your brother goes to prison. I'll make it my mission to see you Indians get nothing, as I always have. Those papers you hold will be forgotten. Oh, there will be a flurry, but nothing will change. We won't remember. We will deny and delay for months. It will be years before anyone acknowledges any wrongdoing, anything improper or ill-advised, a mistake. People are too busy tending to their own affairs to care about anybody else, especially a bunch of red niggers. That's what I know and count on. It's my verity. Human nature is based solely on self-interest. I still hold all the power in this hand." Kraul gestured in Boudinot's face with his fist. "My hand, you misbegotten bastards." Defiantly he shook his hand at the others.

Boudinot listened carefully. His eyes never left Kraul's twisted face. When Kraul had finished, Boudinot looked up at Ira Wolf. "Which hand?" he asked the enraged sycophant.

Kraul slammed his spread hand down on the table. "This one, you bastard."

Before Kraul could withdraw his hand from the table, Wolf gripped the hatchet and drove it down across the hand into the table top, severing the last two fingers.

Kraul wailed and shot up out of the chair as the pain and realization hit him.

In the next room, Mari whirled at the scream, trying to peer through the louvers. "God Almighty," she whispered. Her hand fell on the doorknob, but she did not turn it.

Chapter Seventeen

Boudinot lowered his head briefly, then looked up. The corners of his mouth were drawn tightly downward. "Bring Doctor Howard," he ordered one of the men. "And get his bag from his compartment." Then, turning his head in the direction of the louvered door, he said: "Miss Marshay, you are needed here." The man had barely raised his voice.

Mari's hand caught the doorknob and turned it. She stopped in the doorway for a moment, taking in the scene. Boudinot sat slumped in his chair. Kraul had fainted from the pain, or the sight of his own blood, or the realization of the irrevocable dismemberment. He lay sprawled over the table. Blood was splattered over the surface, and the severed fingers lay at its center, next to the edge of the hatchet that remained where it had penetrated into the wooden table top.

Mari shoved Boudinot's shoulder. "Put more wood in the fire . . . get the poker red hot." As the Indian rose without protest, she looked about for a cloth to stanch the flow of blood spilling Kraul's life out onto the table and the floor. She gathered the towels quickly from the small kitchen and began to wrap them over the wounds, applying pressure to the bloody stumps as well as to the arteries in Kraul's wrist. She raised Kraul's arm above his head. He protested, but without any strength. The front of her white shirt and her skirt became covered with the man's blood.

Meanwhile, Boudinot gripped the poker with a wad of rags and punched it in the fire that he had built up, jabbing and turning the poker as he watched the woman's sure efforts. His blue eyes narrowed slightly as the blood continued to flow even in an extended upright position. He watched as Mari's fingers shifted to the artery in the upper arm.

Phillip Howard entered without haste. "Well, this is a pretty picture, Boudinot. Have you taken to mutilation of your prisoners like your ancestors?"

"Commentary is not necessary, Doctor. Just do what you've been trained to do," said Boudinot, still turning the poker in the coals. "I'm sure Miss Marshay would appreciate some assistance."

"All right. You and you," Howard barked to the remaining guards, "get me a door or something to put this man on."

The guards looked to Boudinot.

"Get the one from the office, there." Boudinot pointed to the adjoining third room.

The men hastened to the other room, returning as Boudinot and Howard were preparing to lift a limp Kraul onto the table. Mari maintained pressure on Kraul's artery as the guards slid the door over the table top while Boudinot and

Howard hoisted up the body. Kraul was placed on the door. Howard slid a chair back under the foot of the makeshift operating surface, raising Kraul's feet slightly. He loosened the patient's belt while checking the color in his thin face.

The hall door to the upstairs chamber opened. A young Indian brought the medical bag to the surgeon. Howard accepted it and turned to Mari. "Has the bleeding slowed at all?" She shook her head. "Is that poker hot, Boudinot?" The 'breed held the glowing point up for the doctor to see. "When I tell you, bring it here." Howard turned to the woman. "Get a tourniquet on him while I examine the wounds."

Mari pulled the scarf from around her neck and wound it twice around the arm before she made the first tie. She picked up a wooden spoon from the table and then placed it on top of the scarf, tying it in place before twisting the tourniquet clockwise with both hands. Meanwhile, Howard checked the flowing wounds. As he worked, he espied the severed fingers lying on the floor. "Planning to make yourself a little necklace, Boudinot? You've got a good beginning, there. I once saw a Cheyenne with a splendid string of fingers. Quite ornamental, nicely done."

"It is the time-honored punishment for a thief," Boudinot responded. "Besides, now Kraul won't be quite so quick to grab what is not his, nor will he ever be able to close his hand so tightly with two fingers missing. He's lucky we didn't cut off his whole hand." He did not like defending his actions to Phillip Howard.

Howard spoke to Mari. "That's good. Tie it off." She bent to the task. "Bring the poker, Boudinot . . . quickly." The Indian crossed the floor in two strides to stand at Howard's side. "Give me the poker and then hold his hand up." Howard looked directly into Boudinot's eyes. "Unless you prefer to torture your victim further by burning him yourself." Boudinot shoved the rag-wrapped poker handle into the doctor's hand as he grabbed Kraul's wrist. Phillip Howard applied the searing iron to the wounds.

Boudinot's nose wrinkled slightly at the smell of burning flesh. His ears would never forget the hissing sound the hot iron made in meeting the moist flesh. Then Kraul began bucking with a piercing scream at the incandescent pain. He thrashed, striking out with his good hand, clipping Mari on her cheek bone. The guards jumped in to help at Howard's command: "Hold him down!" As they all struggled to restrain Kraul, Boudinot threw a punch into the shrieking man's jaw. He fell back.

"Well done!" exclaimed Howard, without glancing up as he completed the cauterization.

While Howard dressed the injured hand, Mari began the clean up. "Throw those fingers into the fire before one of these heathens retrieves them,"

Howard ordered. She wrapped the fingers inside a cloth and tossed the bundle into the fire. The doctor completed his task as Boudinot watched closely. Mari brought water and rags and began to wash the patient's arm and the surface around him. The water in the basin became tinted with the blood.

"Bloody business you are in, Doctor Howard," Boudinot observed.

"Bloody business you caused, Boudinot." Howard snapped down his sleeves over his freshly washed hands.

"Do you have a clean shirt?" Mari asked Boudinot.

"Billy, bring a clean shirt from the bunkroom." Boudinot's eyes remained on Mari as she and Howard lifted Kraul's upper body and cut away the blood soaked shirt. She finished washing Kraul just as the young Indian returned with the garment. Boudinot took it and handed it to her. For a moment their eyes met, then she busied herself trying to slip the shirt on the unconscious patient. That completed, Howard lay the man back. Mari buttoned the shirt and covered Kraul with a blanket she had retrieved from the sleeping room. With the assistance of the guards, Kraul was moved to the small office at the far end of the adjoining rooms.

Mari waited near the door for the men to complete the transfer. Boudinot stood at her side.

"You look very tired, my dear," he said softly, touching the bruise on her cheek. "If you would like to bathe and rest, I will have someone sit with your patient."

"She stays here," Howard said, pushing past Boudinot and into the interrogation room. "The patient is in there, Miss Marshay."

Mari entered the room where they had placed Kraul. She looked closely at the unconscious man, then dropped into the room's only chair, placed her feet on a pulled out drawer, and prepared to watch the patient through the remainder of the night.

"You treat her shabbily, Doctor. She is not your servant," observed Boudinot. "I think you assume too much."

"She knows her work, and everything that goes with it. The rest is none of your damn' business, Boudinot. I've had enough of you, without romantic advice. Mari is not your concern."

Boudinot sighed. "You are correct for the moment, at least," he agreed. "The train is now my concern. I must make arrangements to get the other passengers out of here. As soon as the train carrying my brother arrives, you must be on your way. I would not want there to be any delay in getting you to the Huxley child. That is the bargain." Boudinot left the room.

Howard found a cigar in his pocket and bit off the tip. Lighting it, he casually observed the two

211

guards beside the door. Through the open office door, he could see Mari. The patient remained unconscious. He walked purposefully toward Mari, passing in front of the guards. He stopped with his hand on the splintered doorjamb. "How's his breathing?"

"Shallow, but steady enough," she said without looking up. "You're in a mess, Doc."

"How do you figure that?" Howard puffed the cigar. "Huxley will make the trade. An express will be sent. Boudinot will get his baby brother back. We'll all go on our way. I'll perform the operation in Saint Louis. It's simple."

"Nothing is simple with Boudinot. He is the substance of shadows," Mari observed.

"Boudinot is just a 'breed. Cutting off a man's fingers! That's the way. For all his education and upbringing, just another 'breed."

Mari looked searchingly at Howard. "Do you believe that, Phillip?"

The man nodded. "Just a 'breed. Nothing more."

"I think he's a great deal more."

Howard smiled ironically. "You would."

Quin Milam rocked Cricket Dawson. They swung lazily forward and back in the polished wooden rocker under the impetus of his booted foot firmly planted in the long open window of the McAlester Hotel. The limp lace curtains fluttered occasionally in the light, night wind. There were bright warm glows of color in the windows of the stores that were still open. Music came pleasantly over the air from a saloon down the street. A crowd on the well-lit porch passed a bottle. Some of them were tipped back in chairs. They were laughing. Back in The Flats, Milam would be making his rounds, he thought. He didn't miss it.

When he had lost the ranch, he'd gone to town, feeling he had exchanged bedding down the stock for bedding down the people. All and all, he preferred dealing with stock. He'd always felt at peace after he'd thrown the day's last feed and stood for a while, leaning on the corral fence to watch the content animals. People were never contented.

"When are we going home?" asked the little girl.

Milam glanced down. "I don't know," he said honestly. "It all depends on the lady."

"What lady?"

"The lady that won you in the poker game. She wants to see things are right for you."

"She don't even know me." Cricket rubbed an eye with a small finger.

"Well, no, she doesn't, not yet. But she's a thoughty woman, and she was expecting you to turn up. She wrote me a letter about you, 'fore I knew about you even." He pulled the envelope from his pocket and displayed it before the child. "See right there"—he touched the words—"she

213

wrote my name. Sheriff Quin Milam. Then . . ."
Milam ceremoniously opened it. He withdrew
the tattered note. He'd read it a dozen times to
himself, making sure he understood the words,
making sure it was from the lady and not a
dream. It still had the slight fragrance of her.
Now he read it softly, inflected the businesslike
missive as a bedtime story to the travel-weary
little girl. " 'Sheriff' . . . that's me . . . 'Among
the winnings from the fatal game at the Bee Hive
was a deed to land on the Clear Fork of the
Brazos owned by Mister Dawson' . . . that's your
pa. 'It is quite a large tract' . . . that's your home
place. 'I do not wish to displace Dawson's
widow or children.' She wants you to have a
home, Cricket. She doesn't know it's just you,
but her heart's in the right place. 'When you have
located them' . . . I done that . . . 'and verified
their situation and true claim to the land' . . . I
done that, too . . . 'to my satisfaction.' We're
working on that, aren't we, baby?" He nodded,
and Cricket nodded sleepily, too. " 'I shall return
papers restoring their title to a substantial portion
of the property. The rest they may rent or
purchase over time at a fair price. Please notify
me of the progress of your inquiry.' We are on
our way to doing that . . . come morning. 'You
may always reach me through my attorney,
Samuel A. Bookman, at One-Two-One-Five
Grande Avenue, Saint Louis, Missouri. A fee for

your efforts and inconvenience on my behalf will be sent. In your debt, Mari Marshay.' "

Milam glanced down at the small head that had fallen forward in sleep. He finished the postscript very quietly, almost to himself. " 'Please sell whatever you can of my effects and give the money to someone in need. Or you may hold it as guarantee for your services in expediting the matters with the Dawson heirs.' " He looked out the window into the night. "There's only one heir, ma'am, and she's just little, more in need of a mother right now than a big old raw ranch. But the time for that will come." His hand, still holding the letter, wrapped around Cricket's small elbow. "I don't need a guarantee for my services. It's been a privilege. But, ma'am, don't let us down."

Chapter Eighteen

McAlester, Indian Territory

"Get up, Marshal!" The telegrapher pounded on the door to the room.

"Hellfire! It's open, come on in," growled the deputy marshal, sitting up in the lumpy bed. His hair stuck out. The big mustache had an odd twist at the corner of his mouth. He smoothed it. "Quit that damn' pounding and get in here." The boy stepped to the end of the bed as the deputy marshal struggled to light the lamp. "Well, what is it?"

"It's a message from the railroad lawyer. Do you want me to read it?"

"Read it, kid," murmured the deputy marshal with resignation, as he crossed his arms over the chest of his union suit.

"'United States Deputy Marshal James Killabrew. McAlester, Indian Territory,'" began the boy. "'All charges against Waite Boudinot have been dropped. Deliver him in your custody to station. Engine will pick him up for safe transport to Three Forks Station at one-fifteen a.m. Please see that he stays on the train. Quentin Morgan, Chief Attorney, Missouri, Kansas, and Texas Railroad.'" The boy looked up into Killabrew's weathered face.

"Shit!" Killabrew swore. "He can't jerk the law around like that." The deputy marshal held his big timepiece. Without standing, he jerked his trousers off the end of the bed and thrust both legs into them as he rose. He shoved the watch into his pocket and reached for his shirt. Dropping back onto the bed to pull on his boots, he glanced up at the telegrapher. "What are you waiting for? The government doesn't hand out tips."

"No, sir." The boy shifted the papers in his hand. "There's more. That was just the first one, sir. For a while there, they were coming hot and thick. The next one is from Judge Parker. Shall I read it?"

"Sure, kid." The deputy marshal nodded with his head on his chest, one boot on now.

"United States Deputy . . . ," the telegrapher began.

"Just read the message, kid."

" 'Charges dropped. Release Watie Boudinot to officials of the Katy Railroad at once. Provide no impediments and be sure that Boudinot is in the hands of the railroad and on his way to Three Forks immediately. Judge Isaac Parker. Fifth District Court.' "

Killabrew shook his head. "Even Parker. I'd never've thought he could be bought. What a world."

"Shall I read the next one?"

"Might as well," said the peace officer with grim resignation.

"'Informed all charges dropped against Watie Boudinot. Release him immediately for transport to Three Forks Station. U.S. Grant, President of the United States.'"

"Shit!" exclaimed Deputy Marshal James Killabrew, jumping to his feet. "Why didn't you say it was the President. That tears it. Shit! Shit! Shit!" Killabrew yanked at the sock on his unshod foot. "That shithead Indian's got the President of the United States sending me telegrams." He danced around, trying to shove his shoeless foot in the boot. "Only telegram I ever got from the President, and it's over that shithead. Not . . . well done, deputy. Not . . . thanks for risking your life and wearing your butt off chasin' badmen. No. Just release that shithead." He dropped back to a seat on the bed, thinking, suspended in pulling on the scarred boot. The foot popped through. "By God, something is up. Watie Boudinot ain't worth all this. Something's up at Three Forks Station. Maybe I'll just find out what it is?"

Quin Milam caught the boy's arm as he came out the door. "What's causing all the noise, son?"

"Special train leaving for Three Forks," the young man said, trying not to say too much. "Soon as Watie Boudinot is on board."

"And who is Watie Boudinot?" asked Quin Milam.

• • •

Watie Boudinot rubbed his unshackled wrists as he climbed aboard the waiting engine. He shrugged off the tightness of his arms and shoulders. Looking over his shoulder at the deputy marshal below, he breathed a half snort, half laugh. His mouth twisted as he turned. "Piss on you, law!" He sneered and shot a stream of urine into the deputy marshal's face.

Deputy Marshal James Killabrew reached a gnarled hand for the young 'breed and pulled him down to the train side, among the guards. "You sorry son-of-a . . ." He bit off the words. "You spit in my face, and you caught a blow for it. But you didn't learn anything, did you? Well, you've called the tune, sonny. Now the piper will be paid." He drove a boot toe into the young 'breed's ribs.

Watie struggled to rise from under the blows of the feet and fists as others joined in the assault on his body.

When the Indian was writhing in pain in a pool of his own blood, the big deputy marshal pulled him to his feet. "Oh, ain't you still a pretty boy? *La-dies' man*." He struck Watie hard in the face with repeated blows.

"That'll be enough, Marshal," a strong voice said as a hand caught and stopped Killabrew's raised fist.

"Who the hell do you think you are, fella?"

Killabrew spat out. "You are interfering with a United States deputy marshal's pursuit of his duty."

"I'm interfering in a beating being administered by officers of the court," Quin Milam answered calmly, without hesitation. "That ain't right now, is it? You want the folks there in the station"—he nodded his head in the direction of the station—"to witness you beating up a man on a public platform?"

Killabrew, as well as the other lawmen with him, shot a glance at the dépôt window. Killabrew cockily responded. "Ain't nobody there to see."

Milam bent to lift the prisoner who had sunk to his knees while their heads were turned away. "Ain't that the way of it, though?" he said, straightening. "You'll try a lot of damn' fool stuff if you don't think anybody's watching. And you get away with it for a long time. But sooner or later, boys, you get caught out. Ain't you heard that character is what you are when nobody's around? Shame on you."

"I could arrest you," said Killabrew.

Milam held Watie Boudinot on his feet, feeling the weakness in the beaten man. He looked straight into Killabrew's eyes. "That'd be a mistake, wouldn't it?"

Killabrew looked at the towering man supporting Watie with one hand. He looked at the sidearm resting on his hip in comfortable reach.

"Damn you, Killabrew," swore Frank Barnes, engineer for the M. K. & T. "All you had to do was get this man on the train. Just do what you've been told."

"All I agreed to do was put him on the train," shot back Killabrew. "I never said in what condition. Anyone, including yourself, could say he resisted. He got what he's had coming for a long time."

Watie sagged in Quin Milam's grasp. Frank Barnes stepped forward to help, bolstering up Watie on the other side.

"Nobody made you the judge of that," Milam said. His eyes were hard and steady on Killabrew's face. "Ain't your job. Ain't professional . . . just one scoff-law beating another no better than him. You're worse 'cause you took an oath to support the law."

Killabrew squared up at Milam's words. "He's my prisoner. I'm delivering him to Three Forks." He shifted to shoulder past Milam and take the prisoner.

"You ain't getting on my train," the engineer, stepping toward the lawman, asserted with grim determination. "If this man dies or any harm comes to the folks at Three Forks, you and your filthy temper will be to blame. I'll remember that. I'll make it my business to remember. I'll see Al Huxley knows it, too."

Killabrew glanced at Quin Milam whose big

hand rested on the handle of his pistol. He spat near Milam's boot and set his hat with a shrug. "Think I might lose this high-paying son-of-a-bitch job?"

"A sorry lawman will stretch rope same as another man," Barnes noted.

"Ha!" Killabrew grunted. "He's all yours." Swaggering, he turned his back and strode off with his companions, throwing an arm around one's shoulder, like a man pleased with a job well done.

"Say, thank you, mister," Barnes said to Milam. "Would you help me get this man up inside the engine. We've got to get out of here right away."

"Sure," answered the Texas lawman. "Can you tell me what's going on here?"

"It ain't to be talked about." Barnes looked both ways to make sure his words were not overheard. "This man is being exchanged at Three Forks for a doctor that is to perform surgery on Alfred Huxley's son. Eli Boudinot, this man's brother, and a bunch of Indians are holding *The Prairie Queen* until we get there with him."

Quin Milam pondered the engineer's words, then bent and scooped up Watie Boudinot. "Do you know if there was a gambling woman from Texas on that train headed for Saint Louis?"

"No, I wouldn't know that," answered Barnes. "*The Prairie Queen* is Huxley's car, and it's headed straight for Saint Louis."

Milam carried Watie up the steep stairs into the engine. He laid him back gently against the wall. "This man's in bad shape." Watie moaned and tried to rise. Milam pushed him back. "You need someone to see to him, and I need to get to Saint Louis. I'm coming along."

Barnes could see the sense of that in the open engine. Neither he nor the stoker had time to tend to Watie or his wounds. "You'd have to hand over that hogleg," Barnes said, looking at the gun Milam wore. "It's a dangerous situation out there. A spark could set it off." Milam's vest opened as he bent over Watie, revealing the badge. "You a sheriff? I don't know about that."

"In Texas I'm a town sheriff. Here, I'm just a man going to Saint Louis, trying to help out."

"My orders are to hand over Watie and let it go at that. No shooting, nothing heroic, just hand him over, and get *The Prairie Queen* and her passengers started to Saint Louis as quick as possible. Can you agree to that?"

Milam nodded as he unbuckled his belt and wrapped it around the gun. "That's what we'll do, then. And this man better be alive." He handed the weapon to Frank Barnes. "I've got to get my gear and some blankets from the station. I'll be back."

"We've got to get goin'," said Barnes to the lawman's back.

Watie groaned.

"Hurry!"

Milam went inside. Barnes looked at the stoker, at Watie whose head wobbled feebly against the wall. He set his cap and dropped into his place beside the window. His right hand rested on the Johnson Bar, the throttle, but he did not push it forward. "Sound the bell, Jim."

As the warning clang began, Milam returned with his gear and blankets cradled in one arm and a little girl in the other. He climbed quickly aboard.

"You can't bring along a child," Barnes asserted.

"You need my help, and I can't leave without her," Milam answered. "Right now, I'm all she's got." He knelt down beside Watie and pulled him flat, using one of the blankets for a pillow to prop up his head and covering him with the other, while the child stood at his side.

Barnes eased forward on the throttle. "Well, keep her away from the fire and the door, then, and say your prayers."

Milam grinned. "You a dangerous driver?"

"Shoot!" said Barnes tugging his cap. "That's the least of our worries."

Chapter Nineteen

The key clicked excitedly as John Skinny leaned forward and began to write. When he was done, he ripped the sheet off the worn tablet and streaked down the platform to where Eli Boudinot leaned against a post, smoking, watching the rain. "It's come," he said, bursting in through the man's contemplation. "They've agreed. Watie's to be put on the engine at McAlester. He'll be here by morning."

A smile twisted up the corners of Boudinot's mouth. He flipped a silver dollar to the boy. "Tell the priest to go up and relieve Miss Marshay with the invalid. Have her wait in the sleeping room. Captain Howard is to remain near his patient."

With his hostage secure and his brother on the way, Boudinot had the leisure now to pursue other interests. The Indian smiled as he ascended the iron stairs and went into the train. When he returned to the station with a tray of fine food and a bottle of wine, he was still smiling. His fringed leather coat, replaced with a dinner jacket, now hung over his arm. Ascending the stairs, he walked past the first door where Kraul and Phillip Howard waited. The guard opened the second door and, with a nod from Boudinot, relieved him of the leather jacket.

Mari slept in the lower bunk. Boudinot smiled as he placed the midnight supper on the table. He sat on the bed very gently and pushed a wisp of hair from across her eyes. Mari stirred, then opened her eyes. For a long moment she did not know where she was. As she sat up, she considered the meaning of this newest behavior of the half-breed.

Boudinot rose, picked up the telegram lying on the tray, and handed it to Mari. She turned it toward the light. "By morning my brother will be here. And we will all be on our way again. Each going our separate paths. I've brought us a late supper, if you care to join me."

Mari stood up and started toward the door. "If you don't mind," she said easily, "I prefer to return to the train with the other passengers. I'd like to bathe and change clothes. Then, I'd like to sleep. I'm very tired from all the activity."

Boudinot stepped between her and the outer door.

Mari's eyes ran over him, searching for his intent, any sign of a threat.

"I have a paradise two days' ride from here. A woman like you would make it complete. You'd have whatever you wanted . . . nothing to fear. You could stay until you wearied of me."

"I'm suddenly very weary of you," Mari said flatly. She turned and walked toward the interior louvered door. Boudinot followed.

"I did not believe my offer would offend The Pagan," he suggested.

"The Pagan has reformed, Mister Boudinot."

"The good doctor?" queried the Indian. "I know there was something between you. Doctor Howard has brought about this change?"

"Sometimes we just come to the end of the line and have to change trains."

"I could make it worthwhile for you, Miss Marshay."

"I'm sure you could," Mari agreed. "But if I have a choice, I'm not staying with you or going with you."

"You find me repulsive because of my Indian blood?" asked Boudinot, imprisoning Mari against the door with his outstretched arms. He did not touch her, but merely placed his hands on the doorjamb.

She felt his warm breath against her cheek as he spoke the words. "No," Mari said honestly, looking into his eyes. "Your blood is nothing to me. I began my career as The Pagan because I forgot I was white. I didn't show the proper respect for my station and racial superiority. I went alone to an Apache ceremony . . . a pagan ceremony. I was gone four days without a proper chaperon. I was a ruined woman. Consequently I am not easily offended, when no offense is meant."

Boudinot studied her face. "A girl's prank made you The Pagan?"

"That's right. Nothing at all. My crime was that I refused to recant. I would not explain. I would not ask for forgiveness for something that I did not feel required forgiveness. It was a matter of faith with me. I thought the people I loved should have faith in me."

"Phillip Howard was one of those?" Boudinot asked.

Mari nodded.

Boudinot's forehead wrinkled. "Do you have faith in me?" he asked. "Do you understand what I'm doing is for a purpose? Do you believe I would treat you well?"

"You have no reason to treat me well, Boudinot. I am a stranger who has fallen into your hands. I am not yours."

Boudinot now pressed his weight against her. Touching her neck with his lips, he whispered: "You could be."

The louvered door burst open against his shoulder. Howard caught the Indian and shoved him back, away from Mari. Boudinot's heel hung against a chair leg. He fell backwards to the raw floor.

Boudinot rose quickly with cat-like agility and presence. He stepped toward Howard. "You should mind your own business, sir."

"That is exactly what I intend to do," the doctor said.

Standing back, Mari watched the two men closely.

Boudinot pushed back the hair that had fallen into his face. "You are fortunate to have Doctor Howard for a protector, Miss Marshay," he said to the woman. "Any other man I would have killed for touching me. But I have promised to return him alive. And I will do it." Boudinot left through the broken door.

"You shouldn't have rushed in, Doc. I could have taken care of myself," Mari whispered.

"You've taken care of yourself long enough. I wish I'd had my gun," Phillip Howard fumed.

Mari frowned, but said nothing to her rescuer.

The two guards stationed in the interrogation room came through the door, caught Howard's arms, and threw him roughly against the wall. One held him securely as the other grabbed Mari and dragged her from the room.

On the landing, Mari jerked her arm free from the man's grasp. He observed her with black eyes, then shoved her toward the stairs. The shoving only caused her to move more sedately, more slowly. She straightened, brushed her skirt, and jerked the front of her short jacket into place. Boudinot stood at the rail of the hallway above, watching her, restraining the guard with a mere glance.

Mari glanced up when the guard backed off. "My trunk, Boudinot . . . and its contents?" she asked.

"Your independence?" responded Boudinot.

She nodded.

"Do you think I am a thief?"

"You are a mystery to me, Boudinot," she said flatly.

"It has been returned safely to your compartment, completely intact except for the damage to the lock. You can do what you think best with Reyneau's fortune."

"And Doctor Howard and his patient? When will they be returned to the train?"

"Kraul will be sent to his compartment as soon as Doctor Howard thinks it appropriate. Preparations for your leaving even now are in progress."

"Doctor Howard will return soon?"

"Doctor Howard must, of course, remain in my custody until the arrival of my brother. Then . . . we will see." Boudinot smiled.

Mari did not like the smile. "You don't intend to harm him?" she said. "Not over that cavalier incident? He was just an old friend assuming aid was needed. What would you have thought of him if he had not struck you?"

"I would have thought he was a prudent man. I have given my word to Huxley that Howard will be on the train when it leaves Three Forks."

"Huxley will expect him to be able to operate on the child as soon as he arrives."

"Huxley is not the problem." Boudinot leaned on the banister. "When my brother arrives,

Huxley will have kept his bargain. It's a matter of faith, isn't it? Howard, on the other hand, has insulted me publicly. How shall I deal with that? Could even a bad man know what is right and do it? Perhaps that also is a matter of faith. We shall see. So good night for now, dear lady." Boudinot returned to the upstairs room.

"Don't call me dear lady, Boudinot," she muttered to herself, descending to the first floor. Mari Marshay was angry, outraged at the evening's events. She disliked her own impotence in the face of them. Seething inside, she paced the floor of the station, ignoring Beecher, the only first-class traveler remaining in the waiting room, the others having long since returned to the train.

"How's the doctor?" he asked the woman as she paced.

"He's made an enemy of Boudinot," she answered.

Beecher watched her—two steps, a turn, three steps, another turn, another series of steps. The wind in the brewing storm outside made a mournful music for her movements.

She turned at last on Beecher. "Why don't you do something?" she demanded.

"Why don't you?" he responded.

Mari blurted: "Because I'm not a man. Because I don't have a gun. Because . . ." She stopped at the words that decried everything she'd fought for and believed. "That's one of the most stupid things I've ever said. The truth is I don't know what to do."

"All I can suggest," Beecher pronounced, "is that you spend some time listening to someone who knows how to handle everything. We've come to the end of our mortal power."

Mari studied the preacher, searching for definite shape to the idea that was gathering at the edge of her thoughts. At last she spoke softly. "I believe you are right. That is the only sensible thing to do, if God is still on speaking terms with me."

Beecher was incredulous, matter-of-fact. "God is on speaking terms with everybody. That's the whole point, isn't it?"

Mari turned from Beecher and walked to the car outside. He saw her climb the stairs of *The Prairie Queen* and turn toward her compartment. With a final look about the deserted room, he sat down to wait for the two remaining men, upstairs.

Chapter Twenty

Phillip Howard pulled the blanket higher up on Simeon Kraul's chest. The man still slept fitfully. Howard noted that his own hand was shaking. The episode with Boudinot had awakened a long hidden anger. Howard fought to control himself. He was not a man for rash actions. He was not impulsive, and he wondered at his thoughts, trying to sort them into place again. What else could he have done as a friend, as a gentleman? He had had to confront the man. He owed that much to Mari's father. Claude Marshay would have done it for him had the situation been reversed. He owed it to Mari. After all, part of the breakup was his fault. He should never have exposed a woman to that environment. Perhaps, in some way, he had sanctioned her actions. Howard contemplated that thought.

"Come on now," Howard encouraged Mari who struggled with her footing as they crossed the rough ground. He held her hand and felt good about it. The other officers were similarly helping the ladies back toward the hidden cañon. "This may be very interesting."

"I suppose, if it were in a theater with lovely, soft, velvet seats," postulated Mari as she turned her ankle when a rock slipped beneath her foot. She concentrated on the path. "Remember doormen who helped you down from your carriage onto a swept and trustworthy sidewalk? How we take for granted the small conveniences of life."

"Oh, buck up, Mari. This is an adventure." Howard held her elbow as they slipped and slid down the escarpment. She laughed as he slipped and caught himself with a hasty move and a small curse.

The Apaches had invited the officers of the garrison to observe one of their dances in reciprocation for an ill-conceived invitation from Major Bowie who, somewhat in his cups, had incorporated a party of the chiefs and their wives into a hop at the post. Although the officers did not dislike the Indians when they were not at war, they had some scruples about meeting the savage Apache as a social equal in their quarters and dancing a quadrille with him. Nonetheless, Bowie had made his invitation and stood by it. Under his supervision, the quarters were cleared of the clutter of furniture, swept out, and decked with boughs of evergreens for the occasion. He secured fiddle and guitar players from his company, and all proceeded. That evening had not gone particularly well. Chief Tabiano had offered to buy Colonel Stowe's wife, Sarah, the cavalry beauty. But apparently no ill will had been formed when the colonel refused the offer of two horses. The Apaches had watched the lines of dancing *Americanos*, experienced the clever fiddle and guitar music of the service band. Perhaps they had enjoyed themselves. At least, they had seen the soldiers in a less dominate mode. Now they had returned the invitation. Hospitality required the soldiers to accept. Their boredom cried out for anything that offered relief from the tedium of the post.

The terrain was rough, and the men and women walked carefully as they topped the rise and began a descent down the side of the ravine. Below was a wide defile running between their hill and an almost sheer rock wall beyond. In it the Indians had built a series of enormous fires from which light bounced off the rock, providing surprising illumination in the shadowed cañon.

Indians ran about the stage area, pursuing activities the whites could not understand, and took to be random and senseless. Other Apaches sat on logs around their large drums.

"Perfect spot for an ambush," joked Major Bowie.

"Shut up, right now," said Bell Mason.

"Don't worry, Bell," exclaimed Bowie, twisting his mustache, "I'll save you from a fate worse than death." Phillip and Mari laughed at the interchange between the two bickerers.

The party proceeded deeper into the natural amphitheater. Suddenly Mari held back, afraid of the scene below her. "This *is* a perfect place for an ambush," she said.

"Come on, Mari. That was just Bowie's idea of a joke," summarized Howard. She took his strong arm and followed the others. They found the trunk of a fallen tree and sat down together. The darkness settled in as if on cue, dimming the lights as at a stage play. The dancers came into the arena.

The Apache dancers were naked except for loincloths, their bodies painted over with white clay. Tufts of feathers were attached to their knees and elbows. Upon their heads were great painted wooden racks that added to the dancers' heights. They stomped softly, toe and heel, to the rhythmic music and the jingles of the bells and metal ornamenting their bodies. The sound reverberated off the walls, pressing incessantly into the listeners' ears, blotting out reality beyond the ravine. The fire leaped higher as the men danced, waving feathers, shaking turtle shell rattles, appendages jingling with each movement. Their painted bodies twisted in the light of the fire, casting giant shadows of birds and beasts and demons on the vertical red wall. Mari felt suddenly as if she could not breathe as the enclosure filled with the heat and noise. The shouts grew louder. The drums became more insistent. Then all stopped suddenly. The dancers went away. Two creatures of myth and madness appeared from different ends of the stage. Brandishing their weapons, they began to move with the drumbeats in an intricate dance made large by their shadows upon the wall.

Mari watched attentively. "It has meaning doesn't it? I mean it's not a social dance like ours. It means something to the Apaches."

Howard snorted. "It means they are superstitious bastards . . . primitives trying to appease some force of nature."

Mari looked at him. "They've lived here a long time. Maybe they know some things we don't, Doc."

"Don't make anything out of it," said Howard. "It's just a savage ceremony."

Mari's eyes returned to the movements. "We have entered an unknown world and cannot begin to understand what it means to these people. But somehow it is part of us, too, part of our beginnings, our journey as human beings."

"Good Lord, Mari," blurted Howard. "You don't have to find meaning in everything. They are just jumping about as they have always done and will always do. Think of it as a novelty, something to tell the grandchildren about."

"What shall I tell them, Phillip, that I went West, when it and I were young, and found an old world, old as time, that I did not understand and returned blithely home without trying to understand. What a fool they should think I was to pass over such a chance."

The two dancers' shouts turned to war whoops. They brandished their knives in thrusts and parries. The great racks on their heads swayed as the drums grew louder, more insistent and compelling.

"We are like Orpheus watching the revels of Hades," whispered Bell Mason.

Major Bowie leaned behind Mari. "I say, Howard, this would be a poor sort of place for the women if the Apaches turned treacherous. May not be the wisest decision to have come."

"Apaches don't rape," Mari said suddenly.

"Says who?" asked Bowie.

"Says Bourke. He's followed their customs rather closely. Seems they are quite prudish," answered Mari.

"I'm getting rather tired of Bourke," acknowledged Phillip Howard. "I really don't think you should be listening to him. He is an enlisted man, ignorant in every way."

"Not in every way," whispered Mari,

leaning against Howard's shoulder. "He is not educated, but he is keenly observant and has quite good sense."

"He's your father's servant," countered Howard.

"That is just his job, Doc, not his identity."

"Howard, the other ladies are becoming quite uneasy," observed Major Bowie.

Mari saw the pale tension in the faces around her. The drums had become louder and louder, drowning out the possibility of conversation or thought. The dancers' gestures now seemed more violent and threatening as they were magnified by the towering shadows on the rock wall. The apprehension was very clear on the faces of the white intruders who watched from the hillside. Howard put his mouth close to Mari's ear. "Start back now, Mari. This could become messy. The other women will follow."

Howard remembered her face. Mari had not been afraid. Her initial caution had disappeared as her mind became absorbed in understanding the events unfolding before her. He and her father had placed her in situations not suitable for a woman. Yes, Howard thought, as a man, he had to acknowledge that he had been partly to blame. She was willful, true, but he could have provided more direct guidance. That was his task.

Chapter Twenty-One

Bent over his pocket testament, Beecher looked up when he heard the sound of boots on the stairs.

"No need to wait any longer, Beecher. Nothing more is going to be happening here," announced Boudinot. "In fact, now that things are moving along so quickly toward a successful conclusion, I need to get my gear off the train. Couple of books I'd hate to lose. I'll walk you back and buy you a drink, preacher," Boudinot offered, his voice sounding husky, slightly humorous. "Preacher Beecher. You ever get tired of that?"

"Yes, I do," replied the minister.

"Well, let's get something with some kick down our throats."

Beecher started to puff, but caught himself. "Not much of a drinker, I fear," he said.

"Good," agreed Boudinot, pushing the clergyman toward the door. "More for me. You will see I get home, eh, Beecher?" The 'breed laughed softly as he opened the door and waited for the other man to pass through. "What a rain!" he commented, as they darted toward the *Queen*.

When they stepped onto the iron stairs, the two saw the light in Mari's compartment go out. "Maybe she will get some sleep," Boudinot said almost to himself. "She's had a rough night. You

240

ever see a really good team, Beecher? Well, when they are working, Howard and Miss Marshay seem to know exactly what the other is thinking." He considered his words. "No, she seems to know what he is thinking, hands it to him just before he asks. Lucky man, that Howard. Maybe she isn't so lucky. I personally think he's a prim-assed *prima donna*."

The men passed down the aisle of *The Prairie Queen*. A gentle illumination from the low-burning lamps made the car seem warm and inviting against the rain outside. The crew, under guard, had already returned to prepare for the departure of the passengers. Jimmy Wing leaned on the window across from the Marns' compartment.

"Just the man I wanted to see," Boudinot said, clasping the boy's shoulder and thrusting him forward toward the lounge. "Drinks and cee-gars are on the house tonight." Wing resisted slightly. "Aw, kid, nobody's going to hurt that little girl or the old man. We're lost men here, not wanton defilers of womankind. That's a good point." Boudinot agreed with himself as he shoved the boy forward. "A man can do something he's not proud of because he has to, but he mustn't lose his center. Right, preacher?"

"Right," Beecher agreed, moving briskly under Boudinot's hardy grip.

The men made their way into the softly lit

lounge. "Lovely," said Boudinot as he seated himself before the image of the "Prairie Queen." "Crites was right. She is a pretty woman . . . no, a beautiful woman, a beautiful pagan woman. No wishy-washy there, nothing tentative. Miss Marshay, The Pagan, is a beautiful woman, too . . . not merely a pretty woman, but beautiful."

Beecher slipped onto the adjoining bench. "Tell me, sir, what is the difference . . . a pretty woman versus a beautiful woman?"

"Ah," sighed Boudinot. "As a *connoisseur* of women, I can tell you quite plainly. A pretty woman has good features, a shapely body. She is attractive, presents herself in a charming way. A beautiful woman, on the other hand, may have those same attributes of attractiveness, but she also has rare intelligence and character. She is attractive not only physically, but mentally. She challenges a man. Calls out the best in him, puts demands on him he may not be expecting or willing to assume.

"My own mother was a beautiful woman. I avoid beautiful women whenever possible. They take too much energy. They tend to get into things. You can't put them on a shelf or a pedestal. They make it an emotional struggle to maintain your manly rôle. Eventually you have to admit you are not the end all and be all of creation, merely an associate. Hard to admit that to yourself, let alone to society. Origin of men's clubs, I think. Only way to get any peace and hold the front.

"Considering women recreational, I've always restricted myself to pretty women, Mister Beecher. Perhaps too many pretty women. Never gave a rat's rear-end for them as people, of course, that's easy with a pretty woman. Can't say I ever had a conversation with a pretty woman. That was not my purpose. In that, as I think about it, I'm a great deal like my brother who prefers his women fat, mean, and not too smart. I don't like fat or mean, but I have avoided smart women."

"What do you think of women, preacher?" Boudinot asked Beecher, taking a sip of the drink Jimmy Wing had set before him and turning to get the minister's response, coaxing him with his stare. "Vile sensual creatures, eh, preacher, pulling us superior beings off course . . . cause of the god-damn fall of the whole human race?" He leaned forward toward Beecher. "Give this man a drink, Wing."

The young man set a glass in front of John Beecher and poured it full. Beecher looked into the amber liquid, turned the cool glass in his fingers as he contemplated his answer. "I've always been confused by women," he admitted. "There are those who see them as lower creatures, responsible perhaps for the fall of man, requiring strict subjugation. Rather hard for me, when I consider that it was at my mother's knee I learned of God and experienced love so like his own."

"That one, The Pagan?" asked Boudinot. "You confused about her?"

"Very much so." Beecher nodded, still turning the glass. "I said services over a man she was said to have ruined in San Antonio, but I've seen nothing that indicates she is the kind of woman that would ruin anyone."

"What'd she do? Break up his marriage . . . ruin his family . . . bankrupt him?"

"No, she . . . well, who knows . . . she broke him financially, at cards, and he killed himself. Maybe he was in love with her. I don't know that. She certainly has not presented herself on this journey as a mantrap."

Boudinot laughed. "Mantrap. How appropriate a word. Just the right image. Bait and iron jaws hidden, ready and waiting to kill, maim, and destroy all freedom and self-respect . . . all independence. Hum, there's a word that keeps coming up tonight."

Beecher was still following his thought as he peered into the tumbler. "Maybe it was his financial situation. Or unrealistic expectations. Maybe he had some other problem. The gossip was that she ruined him. Nobody was more explicit than that. I'm afraid I made a conclusion from that phrase and nothing more."

"You're an odd duck for a preacher," Boudinot said appreciatively. "Never thought I'd hear one admit he had made a mistake. Never thought I'd have a drink with a preacher." Boudinot took the glass of untasted whisky from between Beecher's hands and drank the liquid before setting it back. He growled at the smooth fire that slid down his throat and moved his own glass forward for Wing to fill again.

"Preachers make mistakes," divulged Beecher. "I've made more than my share. Generally when I rely on my own incompetent will and judgment. Sometimes I forget my job is not to judge, but to love."

"Now there's a word that is sorely abused, Beecher. I've had a lot of women, but never loved a one. Ain't sure I know what love is?"

"No, not many of us do. Most men substitute making love for love. The word takes on a tinny, hollow quality from so many casual liaisons. In my work on the other hand, love becomes a cloud of fluffy froth . . . too often meaning nothing more than a sappy tolerance for anything and everything. Neither are very good options."

"So what in hell does it mean?" asked Boudinot through the growing warmth of the alcohol he had consumed.

"I'm not sure I can tell you, my friend. Love is important enough to be made the foundation of everything in my faith, though often forgotten.

Think about that. We believe that love is the very nature of God, not vengeance or punishment, but love. Can't be sappy sweet. Can't be mere pro-creativity . . . that only insures continuance. No," Beecher sighed thoughtfully. "It must be something more."

"I live in suspense at your answer," muttered Boudinot. "Let's skip the transcendent stuff and get to the passion."

Beecher smiled. "You are a great skeptic, eh? You've just more or less told me that passion is a vacuous dish if served without substance. Between a man and a woman, I think, love recognizes a partiality made complete in another. The missing parts found."

"Oh, yeah," agreed Boudinot. "I know those parts."

"They are not physical parts, sir," explained Beecher.

"What other parts are there, preacher?" Boudinot concentrated.

"The part that makes you wish to save your brother."

"That's my job. I'm the big brother."

"No, that's your hunger. You want good for him. You see him separate from yourself, but finally whole, complete, his best self. You see the needs that drive him away from it and seek to intervene on his behalf. You've taken us all at great peril to your own future to give him an opportunity to change. In loving him, you become more a man yourself . . . more vulnerable, but truer. It's that way with a man and a woman, also. With the right combination, you are both more than you are alone." Beecher rose from the stool. "I think I'll lie down for a while." He padded off.

Boudinot remained at the bar. He turned to view the chair where Mari had sat during the night she talked with Phillip Howard about their past. "Howard, you're a stupid, ignorant, timorous son-of-a-bitch." Boudinot turned back to the painting, studied it intently. Then he got up slowly and moved to the chair and sat in it. He leaned back and put his hand very gently on the arm. "But then so am I . . . stupid, ignorant, timorous. No time for these thoughts." *Watie is coming. We will begin again, better this time,* he thought. His eyelids felt heavy; he nodded under the watchful protection of the man with the shotgun at the door. Boudinot slept.

Chapter Twenty-Two

It's a matter of faith . . . a matter of faith. Boudinot's words, echoing her own, ran back and forth through Mari Marshay's mind. *A matter of faith. Everything was a matter of faith,* the woman thought. Faith the sun will come up and go down so that you plan the next day—faith that spring will follow winter so that you plow a field and plant it—faith that there is goodness so that you don't despair before evil. Faith even a bad man will keep his word. Faith a man will act true to his nature. When that faith, the substance of hope, is gone, relinquished to circumstances, you are empty, directionless, a wreck creaking in misery on the rocks of life.

A matter of faith. Faith, hope, love. Love is greater. The words and thoughts tumbled through her mind, echoing the training of her youth. Her love for Phillip Howard had not been greater than her discomfort, and finally rebellion, before his critical gaze. She had needed his faith in her soul and spirit. And he could not give it without knowing that he was imperfect, incomplete. Phillip Howard never doubted that he was above other men and certainly women. He was never imperfect or incomplete. Carrying this burden was his purpose, his reason for being.

Mari watched the rain through the window,

washing the grime from the side of the car, streaking the glass. Somewhere she had gotten over Howard. She had found her wholeness, her own self-respect. She sighed. Her eyes followed a rivulet of rain down the glass. Knowing her needs, could she love Phillip Howard for what he was? And if she could, what kind of love would it be?

Her fingers traced over the window, feeling the coolness of the rain beyond. Two ragged streams of rain ran down the pane.

Two ragged streams twice a week. Ration day. The Apaches formed in lines behind their chieftains to receive the government goods. Bored with the outpost, the officers' wives went down to see the ceremony that the Indians took so very solemnly. And so the white women walked casually, sure of their superiority, sure of the protection of their own armed men among the Indians. The Apache women watched them and spoke unknown, disparaging words among themselves. The white women scrutinized the Indians, noting the dirt and dishevelment.

"My God," the cavalry beauty, Sarah, said as she observed the young and handsome chief. "He's all but naked!"

"What legs he has," answered Bell Mason admiringly. "And how he watches Mari."

Mari dropped her eyes at the comment. "The children are so beautiful," she said. "Such luminous eyes. What is at the back of those dark, unfathomable depths?"

"If Diablo has his way," commented the beauty, "you can have a black-eyed child of your own."

"Oh, stop that, Sarah," spoke Bell Mason. "You're just peeved because he's the only man on the post that is not absorbed with you."

"*Gadz,* look at this horror," the beauty pointed. "Is it a disease, Mari?"

The old Apache woman's face was leathery and lined. Her nose was grossly disfigured, the tip cut away revealing the opening into the nasal passage. Mari tried not to stare, being the little doctor her father had trained. She looked instead at the enlisted man that accompanied them. She redirected the question. "Bourke?"

"She is an adulteress," the man explained. "The Apaches cut off a woman's nose for infidelity."

"Oh, watch yourself, Sarah," chuckled Bell Mason.

"How disgusting!" huffed the cavalry beauty.

Mari knelt beside one of the children. The little girl's hand was swollen and red. Mari looked up at the mother. "May I look at your daughter's hand?"

The mother drew the child to her and held her arm tightly across her chest. Mari looked down at the dust and started to rise.

"Look at the child," a low voice said in Spanish as another pair of moccasins stepped into Mari's view. She raised her head to see the face of Spanish Woman. The Apache matron, medicine woman and mother of Diablo, was small and strongly built. The features of her dark face were flat and wide. She carried herself with pride and a dignified presence.

The mother released the child to Mari. Mari smiled and took the girl's injured hand gently in her own. "Oh, that must hurt," she said in Spanish. She looked back at Spanish Woman. "I have some medicine that would make the child's hand better."

Spanish Woman studied the woman kneeling beside the child, gently stroking her arm. The Apache woman's face was impassive, unreadable. She looked at the women with Mari, at Bourke, back at the child, and then at Diablo, the chieftain who had turned to view the disturbance among his people. He nodded at Spanish Woman.

Spanish Woman reached down and took the child's shoulder. "You may heal her hand," she said to Mari.

Mari rose from the dust and walked with Spanish Woman, the mother, and the child toward the shade of the infirmary. *"Siente se."* She sat them under the sparse tree and retrieved a basin and towels along with a small set of tinted bottles, a handful of instruments, and a roll of bandages. Very gently she washed the small hand. "Oh, there it is," she said softly to herself. "A thorn . . . broken off." She turned to Spanish Woman. "I will have to pull out the thorn. It will hurt."

Spanish Woman nodded and spoke in Apache to the little girl who drew herself up to withstand the pain.

Mari smiled. "It won't hurt that much." Without hesitation, she opened the wound and pressed a pair of tweezers over the thorn and withdrew it. "There!" She held up the fragment for the child to see. "Such a big thorn. Such a little hand." She washed the wound with the contents of one of the bottles and watched the suppuration boil out. Repeating the process several times, she then dried the wound, dressed it with iodine, and wrapped it. When she had finished, she gave the two small bottles to Spanish Woman. "It would not hurt to treat it for a few days," she said.

The Apache woman took the bottle. "We will come back tomorrow."

Mari nodded. "I will be here." She pulled a stick of hard candy from her skirt pocket and handed it to her little patient. "*Tu eres una muchacha muy bonita.*" When she looked up, Diablo was standing beside Spanish Woman.

"Move on now," Phillip Howard said from behind her. "You've got your doctoring and candy. Move on."

The Indians shuffled away. Mari turned to Howard. She was frowning. "That was rude, Doc."

Howard ignored her. "Filthy bastards. Mari. I don't want you mingling with these people. I know they are a curiosity, and you're bored, but they don't understand that a kindness is just that. Nothing more. It's like feeding a stray dog. They'll start to hang around. I don't want that. They're all diseased and great thieves. Stay away from that buck. He's no toy." Howard went back into the infirmary, saying over his shoulder: "We need some bandages rolled."

Mari leaned her head against the glass. Phillip Howard was always so sure, so quick to judge a situation and discard the cumbersome emotions. Yet, he was a good and honest man. He was a surgeon of rare ability. But, she thought, he knows only the tissue and bone, nothing of the human being beneath his blade. Had she hurt him? Or had she merely embarrassed him before his friends, offended his sense of propriety? Perhaps she had done both, and more. Phillip had given her a greater degree of his emotional life than she had ever seen him give others. It was a fragile and tentative emotional life, atrophied from disuse or denial, but it was what Phillip offered her. And she had crushed it before it could grow. Mari sighed. That she hated.

"Doctor Howard," the attendant whispered at the door of the infirmary. "Doctor Howard, Miss Marshay is coming across the parade ground."

Howard rose and walked to the door. His eyes focused on the woman. Beyond her, at the edge of the rocks, a young Apache buck waited. The doctor's hand tightened on the doorpost as she waved to the man. "Go and see if she's injured, Schmidt." Howard watched for a few minutes as the soldier ran across the wide, empty field, then he returned to his desk and the report he was making. His thoughts would not focus on the task, but compelled him to turn back to the door, to watch Schmidt reach Mari. They spoke, standing together on the parade, then the two walked toward the infirmary. Howard turned back to his desk and forced himself to work on the papers before him. He heard them enter, the attendant and his own fiancée. Mari came to him and threw her arms around his neck from behind.

"Oh, Phillip, you won't believe what I have to tell you. It's fascinating."

Howard took her hands and removed them. "That will be all, Schmidt. You can check the ward now."

Mari's eyes darted over his face, trying to read the impassive expression. "What's wrong, Phillip?"

"You've been gone four days, Mari. The whole post has been looking for you. We've looked everywhere . . . been through the Apache villages a dozen times. Colonel Wood is still out. Your father is desolate."

Mari turned her head slightly. "And you, Phillip, how are you?"

Howard walked away. "I'm fine now. I'm glad you are back safely."

Reading the coolness, Mari said: "I left a note."

"There was no note," Howard stated.

"I explained everything. Spanish Woman took me to see the girl's ceremony. It was extraordinary . . . like experiencing the origins of human purpose and history."

"Well," Howard said. "I'm glad you enjoyed yourself. You've been a great deal of trouble to everyone here. And with this last bit of brass . . . this parade through the middle of the camp with every eye watching . . . you have also embarrassed me before the entire post."

"You'd rather I was dead at the hands of the Apaches."

"Not dead, no. You should not have gone, Mari. It has ruined everything between us."

Mari studied Howard's back. She walked to him, fixing herself before him so he could not avoid her. "What's wrong?"

"What's wrong? What's wrong? You've been gone four days, Mari. Four days during which time we thought you were abducted, killed . . . who knows what? Now it turns out you just went off to be with the Indians, or should I say with one Indian, Diablo?"

"Diablo?" she whispered, puzzled. "Diablo has nothing to do with this. I went to see the girl's ceremony with Spanish Woman. My God, Phillip, it was an honor, a privilege to be invited, to see what very few white people will ever see . . . to be trusted."

"An honor! A privilege! A disgrace is what it is, Mari. Who knows what you did? You've disgraced me!" Howard shouted in her face.

"What nonsense!" Mari shouted back. "What rubbish! You know I wouldn't disgrace you."

"Do I?" Howard exclaimed. "Do I now? It's for sure no one else will believe that."

"You want to call the marriage off?"

"That seems appropriate."

"Fine."

"What's that in your hair?" Howard asked abruptly.

"Pollen."

"Good God! Fertility ceremonies! Heathen! Pagan!" Disgust was pungent in Howard's voice and posture.

Anger erupted from the girl. "Then forgive me, you pompous, obtuse, superior, sanctimonious son-of-a-bitch, I am but a pagan."

Mari left the infirmary and walked quickly back to the cottage-like *jacal* she shared with her father. She noticed that the wives of the officers had come to their doors and porches. No doubt they had heard the shouting. Now they watched her with arms folded. She had betrayed them, too, broken the bond. Their men had gone out, possibly risking their lives, for nothing. It was not done. It had turned out Mari was not a victim, but the perpetrator of a hoax. She had violated her membership in the military family by allowing them to risk their lives while she was on a lark of a questionable nature. Mari's eyes caught a glimpse of the cavalry beauty, Sarah, lifting her lovely nose and retreating inside her house. The other women also went inside, even Bell Mason. Howard was right. Mari was disgraced.

At her door, Dr. Marshay embraced his daughter as tears ran down her face and his. He kissed her forehead and held her tightly. In his arms, she wept.

"Oh, Papa, I've made a mess of things. Phillip thinks I . . . ," she choked out at last.

"Phillip's an ass," her father said. "Maybe it's for the best."

But the ache in Mari's heart did not think it was for the best.

Mari Marshay felt the pain as if it were fresh. She felt the guilt, not of her disgrace, but of destroying Howard's feeble first emotional steps.

A confident knock on the door pulled her back from the morbid thoughts. She gathered herself for a moment, then wiped the tears from her cheeks and went to the door. Boudinot leaned against the wall. There were deep circles under his eyes. His shirt collar was unbuttoned and twisted underneath the wrinkled dinner jacket. He smiled.

Her head tilted slightly. "You are not going to start that nonsense again?"

"Dear lady, I'm a perfect gentleman . . . from time to time." He placed his hand over his chest, swayed slightly. "May I come in?"

She backed into the room, allowing him access. She did not close the door, but stood beside it.

"Ha," Boudinot laughed. "I have not come for

your honor, Miss Marshay." He looked at the chair. "May I sit?" She nodded. He sat down, looking about the small room. "Well, why don't you sit down, too. Then, we can talk."

"What do we have to talk about, Boudinot?" Mari sat on the edge of the bed.

"Oh," the man observed. "We could begin with the weather. Awful, isn't it?"

"I like rain." She continued to sit silently, enjoying in a way his discomfort.

"Then, perhaps, you could tell me about yourself. You were in New Orleans during the war?" She nodded. "Interesting, so was I. You can talk, too. Feel free to enter in at any point."

Mari sighed. "What were you doing in New Orleans?"

"I was dying on a cold wet pavement . . . dumped there with a hundred other men . . . until someone noticed I wasn't dead and treated my wounds. But I was never able to say thank you. By the time I recovered, the doctor was gone. It has haunted me. I still wake up feeling the cold, my life slipping away, and then the warm touch of the healing hand making me live again."

Mari nodded. "Well, that is poetry, Boudinot. Any doctor would be pleased to know that his efforts had made you live again."

"It's true. I knew death and life that night."

"I've often wondered what the dying feel and see."

"Oh, things are very clear," supplied Boudinot. "Extreme clarity, acuity. You know we've slept together before."

Mari stood and turned to him so quickly the garnet earrings, hanging from her ears, swung wildly. "Don't you even say that, Boudinot. I have a great many vices, but I am not careless about men. I know I have never slept with you."

"Oh, yes." Boudinot was pleased at her irritation. "I was innocently lying there, and you crawled right on top of me. What could I do? It was your idea."

"Never."

"Yes, it happened. Maybe you don't recognize me now. I had a beard then."

"Never," Mari repeated.

The smile faded from Boudinot's face. "I was freezing from the inside out. You and two black men carried me out of the rain and fog and washed me with warm water and dried me. You took the metal fragments from my body and sewed me back together. You put heated blankets on me, but it was not enough, I was still shivering, so you crawled against me and slept there through the night. When I awoke, warm again and alive, you were gone. I waited for you. Dreamed about you. But you never came back. Jeter told me that you had been dismissed for saving me and then sent away. He did not know your name . . . just missy. You saved my life, Miss Marshay. Today I am grateful."

Mari sat back, remembering. "That was a long time ago."

"You're a good doctor. Better than Howard probably."

"I'm not."

"Maybe he thinks you could be. Maybe that's why you can't quite get along."

"That's not your business, Boudinot."

"Right now my business is anything I say it is," the 'breed said. He looked at his hands. "Part of my family lives in Philadelphia. I have not been to see them in some time. Estranged, I suppose, wrong side in the war. But white or red, they are our people, are they not? The events of the last few hours, you . . . well, I was thinking . . ." Boudinot was self-conscious, strangely awkward. "There is a medical school there . . . in Philadelphia. I heard they are accepting women . . ."—Boudinot looked at Mari for some support—"to train as doctors. When I first heard about it, even after New Orleans, I thought it was a joke. Women in medicine and all that." He hesitated. "But you should go there. You are too good, probably too hardheaded, too, to take orders from somebody else. Howard's a good doctor, but you are 'way ahead of him. You don't need to ride double. You need to take the horse by the bit and ride where you ought to be."

Mari leaned back against the seat and crossed her arms. "Where is this going?"

261

"Well, you've got your independence." Boudinot patted the little trunk with the broken latch. "You're through gambling, and I'd guess you're also through with whatever you ran away from during the war . . . 'cause you're back. Maybe you're ready to become a doctor on your own."

"Maybe."

Boudinot's face twisted into a smile, contemptuous of his own vulnerability. "Well, maybe I'll visit Philadelphia sometime. If I do, I'd like to see you. I can occasionally behave myself with a woman, even if I appeared to be too forward with you upstairs."

"Is that an apology?"

"Yes, it is." Boudinot's voice softened. He became serious. "I'd like to know I'd be welcome."

Mari sat, sorting the ideas Boudinot had placed in her mind.

A whistle screamed in the distance, warning of the approaching train. At the sound the lawyer jumped to his feet. "Think about it," he said as he hastily left the compartment to prepare for the arrival of Watie Boudinot.

Chapter Twenty-Three

Simeon Kraul was awake. "I'll kill that arrogant Indian," he hissed. "No, I'll do worse. I'll destroy him and let him live with it."

"Forget that, Kraul," Howard interrupted the man's ridiculous thoughts. "You did the crime. All things considered, you could have been treated worse. I think that if you'd robbed people I was responsible for, I might not have settled for two fingers. Next time you might not be so lucky."

"Lucky?" blurted Kraul, before settling into a sinister smirk. "Take his side then, Doctor. You're not beyond reach. Your solicitations won't be appreciated, I can assure you. These aborigines are a different class of beings . . . nothing in the scheme of things. They'll never have any power. They don't understand it. Power is what the world bows to, not goodness or need. Just power. They aren't the kind of men that can understand that or use it. They are too simple, too primitive. They just want their little lives."

Boudinot appeared at the door. "Can he be moved back to the train? It's almost dawn. The engine is arriving."

Howard turned. Boudinot leaned with his white shirt rumpled, the stiff collar unbuttoned. His hair fell over his eyes. *He's paid a price for this night.*

The realization rushed through Howard's mind.

"Yes, he can be returned to the train. Father Reyneau should remain with him until we are under way. Then, Mari or I will be there."

Boudinot turned his attention to the prone traitor. "So, Kraul, you've come out alive and are on your way back to civilization. If I were you, I would not crawl the Bridge again." He smiled. "There will be a warm reception waiting for you in Saint Louis. It should be quite stimulating."

Kraul shook his head.

"Don't be modest," Boudinot stated. "It is no more than you deserve. It was my pleasure to have arranged it for you."

"You sent the telegrams?" Simeon Kraul's eyes narrowed to thin slits.

Boudinot nodded. "Not all of them. But you are expected. Sending your confession has taken the telegrapher some time."

"You think you've beaten me," whispered Kraul.

Boudinot met the man's burning eyes without flinching. "No," the 'breed said softly. "Men like you are not beaten in this world. I may have deflected you or delayed you, but you will continue your course. Just don't attempt to do it here. Billy, Two Eagles, take this man back to his compartment."

Boudinot returned to the interrogation room as Reyneau and Kraul were escorted back to the train. Outside, the rain poured down harder, darkening the approaching sunrise. It slapped the frame building, here, there, with the erratic force of the inconstant prairie wind.

Mari sat on the bed, still thinking about what had happened. If Howard was a captive of his confident superiority, what was Boudinot? Was he a vengeful renegade who extracted a bloody punishment for the breach of his law? An idealist who believed in justice and fairness, in keeping your word, while at the same time denying the ideal as impractical in the world of men? A man who loved his worthless brother so much he would risk his own future and the lives of all onboard *The Prairie Queen*? A romantic who wanted to court his chosen woman with gentility and thoughtfulness? Did his treatment of Simeon Kraul offer any clue? How was she to read his actions toward her—his tolerance, his respect, his proposition in the bunkroom, the easy way he surrounded her, filling her with confidence, not fear? Had he, too, dared to reveal his hidden heart?

She sighed at the complexity of the man and the circumstances. It was almost over now. Everything was arranged. Only the final happy act remained, when Watie Boudinot would be returned and the passengers would be again on their way. Howard would return safely to his world. Boudinot? What would become of Boudinot? A short time ago she would not have wondered, not have cared. Now she saw an image of the two men walking up to the very edge of a sheet of thin ice, and then beyond. She told herself, if nothing went wrong, in a little while it would be over. A shudder ran through the woman—*if nothing went wrong.*

The whistle blasted through Mari's thoughts. When she opened her eyes, she noticed the first light of dawn was dispelling the darkness. She stood and slid back her door. Through the side windows, she saw Boudinot. He leaned with forearm above his head against one of the porch posts. Appearing casual, he was nonetheless fixed on the arrival of the engine from McAlester. There were other men on the porch, men with guns cradled in their arms. He straightened as the engine eased into the station. She saw his eyes searching for his brother, for Watie.

Watching Boudinot, Mari knew something was wrong. She stripped off her robe and quickly dressed. Running through the aisle of *The Prairie Queen*, she pushed past Simeon Kraul and the men assisting him into his compartment. One of the men caught her arm. She jerked it away.

"Let me go!" she said with the authority of need. The Indian released her.

On the iron platform, Mari encountered two guards with guns grasped, ready for any treachery. Mari could not see around them. She pushed and was pushed back. She strained to see.

Peering around one of the guard's arms, she saw a figure jump down from the engine. Soon the engineer and stoker gently eased another man into his strong grasp. Mari knew the big man on the ground from Texas, Sheriff Quin Milam. *How curious?*—the words flickered across her mind. Milam caught the man's arm as his stumbling feet faltered in the mud. Boudinot came off the porch toward them. Something in a blanket was handed to Milam, he shouldered it, and walked splashing through the water toward the station, carefully guiding the second man. The engineer caught up the weak man's other side. Boudinot was shouting above the rain as they met.

Mari ducked under a platform guard's arm. She sprinted for the building and dashed toward the stairs. The inner guards were gone.

"Phillip," she called out, flying up the stairs ahead of the men outside in the rain.

"Here," Howard said.

"Something is wrong. Something has happened. Watie Boudinot is injured. You've got to get out of here, get to the train, somewhere public."

Howard caught up his bag and followed her. They tore down the hall and stairs. Mari was still on the staircase when Boudinot and the other men entered. She stopped suspended in flight. Water ran off their hats and bodies onto the mud-tracked floor. Boudinot's attention was not on the stairway, but on his brother's ashen face.

"What happened?" His words were soft but full of anger.

"I can tell you that later," answered the big Texan. "Right now this man could use some medical attention, or at least a bed. He's coming and going from the thumping his head took."

Boudinot looked up then at the stairway and saw Howard and Mari. His blue eyes narrowed. "We have both. This way, sir."

Quin Milam and the engineer started toward the stairs. Watie sagged. Boudinot pushed the engineer aside and took his place. Milam looked up the stairs. Seeing Mari, he smiled as if it were a sunny day without crisis boiling around them.

"You are here, ma'am. That pretty near makes my day." Then he glanced at Watie and Boudinot, struggling on the steps. "Here, take this." He offered her the blanket wrapped bundle. Mari accepted it. "She's asleep. Worn out from being dragged around." Starting to recognize the form as a child, Mari stepped aside to let the men pass.

"This ain't working," the lawman observed as Watie sagged again within their grasp. "Here." Milam reached down and lifted Watie into his arms and climbed the stairs with Boudinot ahead of him.

As he opened the door for Milam to enter,

Boudinot turned back to Howard and Mari. "Your departure has been delayed . . . indefinitely. Will you come willingly or should I have someone assist you?"

Howard looked at Mari and shrugged. He went up the stairs, then turned back impatiently. "Put down that papoose and come and help me."

Mari looked down at the little girl whose head had emerged from the blanket. "It was so simple," she whispered, looking through the muddy lobby at the sheeting rain beyond the open door. "A matter of faith. Watie would be returned, and *The Prairie Queen* and her passengers would be on their way again." She spoke softly to no one but herself.

"It was not the railroad, miss," Frank Barnes said beside her. "We done our part. It was that Marshal Killabrew. Watie defied him. That's what done it. The marshal don't take nothing. That's his rule."

"He took something tonight," the woman said sadly.

"Said he agreed to return the Indian like everybody wanted, but he did not say in what shape. That's hard, ain't it, ma'am?"

"Hard, indeed," Mari agreed. "The technical excuse, the permission to justify an evil deed. Everybody has to get his part of the pie cut just a little larger. Nobody ever thinks about what it does to the next man. Would you take the child to my compartment and ask Louise to watch her until I return."

"She's a nice little girl. Guess nobody is leaving right now." Barnes took the child and started back to the train. Mari climbed the stairs slowly, thoughtfully.

When she entered the interrogation room, Watie was sitting, with Milam's help, on the door atop the desk where Kraul had been. Howard stood across the room. "Take your time, Miss Marshay. No hurry here. This fool won't let me touch his brother."

"Shut up," snapped Boudinot. "See to your patient, Miss Marshay."

"What the hell do you have in mind?" Howard demanded.

"I said shut up." Boudinot was calm but deadly. "Right now I'm fighting a terrible urge to kill you."

Howard subsided in his tone. "I'm a doctor, man. It's my duty to see to his injuries."

Boudinot's face twisted. "A man of duty left me to die. She saved me. She'll save him. Your days as a doctor are over, unless she needs you to do something."

A chill ran down Mari's back as she tried to read Boudinot's dark face.

"Well," he jerked the bag from Howard and handed it to Mari. "Do it."

Mari went to Watie. She turned his face into the

light. Milam continued to hold the man erect. She unbuttoned the single button still holding the young breed's bloody shirt together. Peeling it back off his shoulders, she studied the cuts and bruises. Watie swam in and out of consciousness. Mari's hands touched his ribs. He winced. Her fingers ran over the spleen and abdomen. Bruised but no rupture, no ghastly stain of blood beneath the skin, no internal bleeding. She unbuckled his belt and pants looking for injury, signs of bleeding.

As she ran her hand along his lower abdomen, Watie reacted. "I'm going to like you, honey. You got great hands," he said, then swam away in unconsciousness.

Mari moved to his back. "You can lay him down now," she said to Milam. Boudinot stood nearby, watching. "I can't give him anything for the pain. His face, his head has taken a severe beating. We will clean him up and wrap the ribs and see what comes next. This is within my abilities, Boudinot. Doctor Howard is not needed to help here. He should go on to Saint Louis. His patient is waiting."

"Elk Stalker, bring a basin and hot water." Boudinot did not acknowledge Mari's words about Phillip Howard.

"I will not continue until Doctor Howard is on the train," Mari said quietly. "He has an extremely ill patient and very little time left."

Boudinot drew the heavy pistol from his belt and pointed it at Howard. "Go on, do it now. Howard's life is in your hands. Ira, hold his hand against the wall." Wolf pinned the doctor's open left hand against the wood, as the other Indians struggled to hold him. Mari hesitated. "Get to work now!" shouted Boudinot, and fired the weapon with a deafening roar. The woman's hand went to her mouth as the smoke obscured her vision. Boudinot shoved her gently toward Watie. His voice was calm in the sudden stillness, as if the gun's percussion had exploded his own anger out of him. "Howard's not hurt . . . not yet, anyway. What you do will determine the rest."

Mari took the steaming basin from Elk Stalker and set it down beside Watie. As she worked, the other men except for Boudinot and Howard began to leave. Howard flopped into a chair and crossed his arms insolently across his chest as he watched. Gently washing the battered and bruised face, she spoke quietly to Milam who helped move the injured man as she wished. She worked intently, silently, for a long time.

"I'll need a sheet, something to make bandages," Mari said to Boudinot. He went into the sleeping room.

Glancing quickly at the lawman, she spoke softly. "Boudinot intends to do something to Howard. If I can arrange it, will you make sure the doctor gets on the train and safely out of here?"

Milam nodded. "I'll back you. But Boudinot is deep mad, ma'am. Be careful what you try. It could blow up in your face and get Howard killed."

"There must not be any killing . . . of anyone. This has been a trial, but, so far, no one is dead."

Boudinot returned with a bed linen.

"Always glad to take an easy hand." Milam took the sheet.

"Tear me some strips about six inches wide," Mari instructed, ripping a section for herself and handing him another. "Like this." Boudinot remained at her shoulder. "You, sir, are in my light. Please sit over there. Your brother will survive in spite of his beating. Trust me." Boudinot's troubled face looked into hers. "Sit down, Boudinot, you don't need to see all of this," she added softly.

As Boudinot went to a chair, Mari glanced in Milam's eyes, then back at her work. "What are you doing here?"

"I brought you Tim Dawson's little girl."

"Dawson . . . the man killed at the Bee Hive? The man whose land I won?"

"That's right. You said to find the heirs in your letter."

"As I remember, I asked you to inform me about the widow and children, not bring them."

273

Mari tore and rolled bandages with practiced speed and skill as Milam's big hands carefully worked on a single roll.

"There's just the little girl. She's alone. I figured you were the closest thing she has to a guardian."

"Quit talking," Boudinot said harshly from his seat across the room.

"Lift him up and hold him." Milam held the 'breed as Mari began to wrap the cloth around the bruised and broken ribs of Watie Boudinot. She pulled tightly even as he moaned. Her eyes found Boudinot sitting at the table. His head was down in thought. His hand rested on the hatchet that had severed Simeon Kraul's fingers. She split and tied the bandage. "Boudinot, may I speak with you in the sleeping room?"

Boudinot rose swiftly. "Is something going wrong?"

"No, not that I can see." She walked to the inner door with Boudinot at her side. His eyes traveled past her face to settle on Howard who sat defiantly, near the other door.

Inside the small room, she turned abruptly to Boudinot. "It's time to send Howard on. You've delayed the Saint Louis surgery long enough. Richard Huxley is my godson. His mother my best friend. You must send Howard . . . *now*."

"I'm not finished with Howard. He has a debt to pay for Watie, for his insult to me."

"I will pay that debt. Take the hundred and fifty thousand from my case."

"It's not enough."

"I can have an equal sum placed in your name within the hour."

Boudinot's arm encircled her waist. She did not draw away. "You know money won't be enough. Your money costs Howard nothing. I will want you."

"You have the cards, Boudinot."

"I have your word?"

Mari nodded.

"I think your word would mean something to you." Boudinot's eyes searched her face, then he stepped away. He opened the door to the main room, allowing the woman to pass in front of him. Walking back toward Watie and Milam, she began to put Howard's medical bag together.

"You may go, Doctor Howard," Boudinot said, standing above him with one hand on his hip, the other on the large caliber pistol in his belt.

Howard rose to his feet. "Thank God, you've shown some sense at last, Boudinot. Gather the things and let's go, Mari."

She closed the bag, rolled down her sleeves, and handed the bag to Milam without looking at Howard. "Go on, Phillip. Richard Huxley needs you now."

Howard looked at Boudinot, then at Mari. "What's going on?"

Mari took a step closer to Boudinot. "Nothing is going on. I will take a later train as soon as Watie is better. A few days, perhaps."

"Quit coddling him," Boudinot said to her but looked into Howard's eyes. "She's buying your hand, your career, if not your life. Accept it graciously like the good little ass you are and go before my distaste for you overcomes my word."

"To hell with that!" exploded Howard. "I won't have it."

"Sure you will." Boudinot walked to the table where he moved the hatchet with the outstretched fingers of his hand. "You've seen what I'm capable of when people don't keep their word. The railroad did not keep their word. I have every right to return you in the same or worse condition. Worse, I think, after that contemptuous little attack on my person earlier in the evening."

Howard paled, but he spoke with surety. "You dare not. An attack on my person . . . any act that prevents me or further delays me from caring for my patient . . . would bring all the forces in Huxley's considerable power down on you."

"What about *my* patient?"

"She's said he will survive."

The two men studied each other. Boudinot let Howard dangle.

"She has told you she will take a later train," Boudinot stated.

"You are holding her against her will."

276

"I am not," Boudinot answered easily. "She's staying of her own volition." His hand rested on the doorknob. He turned it to open the door. Then he smiled a twisted smile. "Pleasant journey, sir. May you always enjoy the full knowledge that she's buying your future with her own. How grateful you must be that this woman would care that much about you. Or does she, Doctor? Perhaps she has found you lacking and prefers a better man."

"I won't leave her," Howard said, raising his chin.

"Very well then, lay your hand there on the table . . . freely without my men holding you."

Howard looked at the blood-saturated table top. "My hands . . . my patient . . ."

Boudinot enjoyed the doctor's dilemma. "Do you not see the open door, the justification for leaving I've just given you? The way to save your hand and your precious ass. Maybe she's not saving you. Maybe she's coming to me. Why would you risk so much when there is a chance of that?"

Howard looked startled, stunned by the words. He frowned. "You can't put thoughts in my mind. I trust her totally."

"My money says you betrayed her once to protect your ego, and you'll do it again to save your hide."

"Get it over with, Boudinot," Mari said. "Quit

playing with him. Go, Phillip. Sheriff Milam, see he gets on the train, please." Milam walked around the end of the table.

Howard put up his hand to restrain the sheriff. "Is it me you're trying to save or is it Boudinot, Mari? Are you staying to protect me or to be with him?"

Mari shrugged, then leaned across the table, holding Howard's eyes. "I'm staying to be with Boudinot, Doc. What would you expect of The Pagan? You have a patient to see. Now go and do what only you can do."

"And that refusal I broke up?"

"You came in too soon, Doc. I was just delaying for effect." Mari slipped her arm through Boudinot's.

"You . . ." Howard bit off the sentence. "I was willing to forgive you, to stand up against this man for you. Well, good riddance to you both." He snatched the bag from Quin Milam's hand. At the door he turned back. Mari Marshay was looking into Boudinot's clear blue eyes. Howard left. Quin Milam tipped his hat to the lady and followed. When she heard their boots on the stairs, she released Boudinot's arm and stepped away.

"Why did you let him off?" Boudinot asked in astonishment. "You know what he is."

"Yes," she said softly. "I do, but he does not."

"And you don't want him to know? I'd want to squeeze his nuts."

"What good would that do, Boudinot?"

"It would give me a great deal of satisfaction."

"It's not satisfying to see a crippled soul. I once loved him. I wanted him to be better." Mari walked to the window and watched the preparations for departure. Boudinot came to her side. Phillip Howard did not look back as Quin Milam put him on board, turned, and walked along the tracks to visit with Fred Barnes.

"Funny man that Texan," observed Boudinot. "The engineer said he stopped the beating, backed down Killabrew and his thugs. Said he tended Watie all the way here. Why would he do that?"

"He's a funny man," Mari said, studying the Texas lawman. "Very funny."

Watie moaned, and Mari went to his side.

Boudinot remained at the window. "He never once tried to interfere here. Not that he could have, of course. Maybe he is smart."

Along the hallway of *The Prairie Queen*, Mrs. Todd stood, arms crossed, in the entry to Mari's compartment. Inside the compartment, Cricket Dawson drew pictures on pieces of paper from Mari's stationary box. Louise sat among the scattered contents of Quin Milam's saddlebag. "Well," the general's wife said huffily to the black woman. "Doctor Howard has returned to his quarters. This train will soon be leaving.

You've barely time to make me comfortable for the journey."

"Yes, ma'am," Louise answered. "You sure do need to get fixed for the journey. I'll get to that, here, just as soon as Miss Mari comes for this baby." Louise looked at the child playing on the floor.

"You must put that child out. She's not your responsibility. I am."

"You is a growed-up woman, Missus Todd. This here is just a little child. I can't put no child out on the platform and leave."

"Why ever not?" asked the puzzled woman.

"It wouldn't be right. I's put in charge of her. I give my promise. Miss Mari will come get her. You'll see."

"It appears *Miss Mari* has shown her true colors and is staying behind with that half-breed, Boudinot. She'll not be back for an urchin like this one."

"Sure she will, Missus Todd. She's quality . . . that woman."

"She's trash!" Mrs. Todd's voice was strong and commanding. "Put that child out now or I shall."

Louise stood above Cricket Dawson, blocking Mrs. Todd with her body. "No, ma'am. I won't and neither will you. You lived above the slave line, so you think you is better than them folkes you whupped. But there ain't a hair's difference between you and that overseer took my little child away from me. You both don't know nothin' about a heart and how it feels to have it ripped out of your body. You just think about what you want same as him. People ain't nothing to you. I am a free woman now. And I am not going back to doin' what God Himself knows is wrong."

"You ingrate. No one ever has spoken to me like that." Mrs. Todd was deeply offended. "I've given you a home. I've treated you well. Paid you fairly. Put up with your insolence. Very well, enough is enough. I shall manage. You are fired, Louise."

Milam knocked on the facing of the open door as Mrs. Todd abruptly turned. "Excuse me, ladies. I overheard some of your conversation. If you truly intend to fire Louise and she is willing, I'd like to hire her."

Mrs. Todd threw a hand into the air, brushing aside such foolish disregard for her own needs. "Take her. I have not further need for her." She flounced down the hall past the Texas sheriff.

"What you doin' draggin' this child all over the country?" asked Louise. "Ain't you got no sense?"

Cricket darted into Milam's arms as he kneeled to pick her up. "Louise," he began, "I may not have much sense. I always thought I did, but maybe I don't. Maybe I been grabbin' straws since Cricket came into my life. But I feel like there is somethin' important going on, even though I'm not altogether sure what it is. A week ago, I was a sheriff in a dirty, little Texas town. Now it don't seem like that was ever a part of my life. I took this child from the undertaker, after her pa was killed. It was my job to put her in an orphanage, but then I remembered that Miss Marshay sort of won her in the poker game where her pa was killed. In my whole life I ain't thought as much about women as I have about these two. I can't get shut of either of them. Now I see clearly what has to be done to put things right, and I sure could use your help."

"You want that white woman to take this child?"

Milam nodded.

Louise's eyes narrowed. "Is that all? You see an easy way to take advantage of her and this child?"

"Tell you the truth, Louise. I don't see anything but a lot of trouble. And I just don't seem to care."

"Set down here and tell me what you-all is thinking." Louise patted the couch.

"It's over." Boudinot left the window as *The Prairie Queen* disappeared down the track. "Howard will get to his patient. Watie will recover. When do you think we can leave for home?"

"The paradise two days' ride from here?" asked Mari.

"You were listening to my proposition," said Boudinot.

"I was listening."

"But not seriously considering."

"I liked the offer of meeting you in Philadelphia better," she said.

"I was more sure of you, then," Boudinot said, and smiled. He took her hand and brushed it with his lips. "Perhaps you will discover . . ."

There was a gentle knock on the door. They turned together. "Excuse me, folks," Quin Milam said around the door. "I've come for the lady."

Chapter Twenty-Four

Boudinot threw back his head and laughed. "Does Texas never run out of fools?" Then his tone shifted. "The lady is mine by choice and by right."

Milam came into the room. "Well, not really. We got our rears whupped learnin' nobody can own anybody else. You're just blowin' smoke, Boudinot, hoping somebody will let you get away with it."

"I have gotten away with it. You're brave, bold, and reckless . . . bearding me in the midst of my men."

"Oh, your men." Milam's tone was not threatening, but easy and conversational. "They went home. When I took Doctor Howard to the train, I told them it was all over and you'd said they'd better clear on out and lay low in case the railroad sent a second train with deputies. Ira Wolf was kind of hurt you didn't tell him yourself, but I said you were staying with your brother. And he said you didn't have good sense when Watie was around."

"You don't have a gun," observed Boudinot.

"No, I don't. Carrying a gun can get somebody hurt. Maybe me. I wouldn't like that. Now let's give this lady a real choice . . . when you don't have your thumb on the scale. You know whatever she's agreed to ain't worth spit, since it was bargained under duress."

Boudinot inhaled deeply. "I'd kill to keep this woman."

"Sure, you would, and she'd probably be worth it, too. But you'd know she didn't come to you freely. And I figure that's the best part of an independent woman like her . . . her free will, not just any port in a storm." While he was speaking, Milam had slowly closed the space between himself and Boudinot. The men were squared off now.

"Stop this," Mari said, stepping between them. "Boudinot must release me from my word or nothing you do or say matters. I am bound by my word."

Boudinot walked away. "I don't want you bound, Mari. That's never what I wanted. It's what I took until there was time."

"Well, there you have it. Boudinot is a man, after all." Milam gestured toward the door. "Bring your things."

"The train has left," Mari said.

"One train has left," answered the lawman.

Mari's eyes narrowed. "Why are you here, Milam?"

"Well, ma'am, we have business, you and I." He removed Mari's letter from his pocket. "You deputized me, so to speak, to carry out a task for you. And I'd like to do that."

"The child?"

"Yes, ma'am."

"Where is the little girl?"

"She's with Louise."

"On the way to Saint Louis?"

"Oh, no. They are just downstairs."

"You got Louise to stay?"

"Well, yes, ma'am. She didn't seem real happy with Missus Todd. And you needed someone to help with Cricket."

"Don't call me ma'am, and don't arrange my life, Milam," Mari said.

"Sorry, if I overstepped," Quin Milam answered humbly.

"Cut the crap, Milam!" barked Boudinot. "Do you expect this woman to take on a child for you without any preface?"

"She won her fair and square in that poker game."

"If you can't own people, as you just pointed out," Boudinot stated, "you cannot win them in poker games, either."

During the exchange Mari Marshay had walked to the door and out to the landing. From there she could see Cricket Dawson, sitting comfortably in Louise's lap.

"She doesn't have any family," Quin Milam spoke at her shoulder. "If I take her back, it's to the orphanage in San Antone."

Mari turned to look at him. "It won't work,

Sheriff. I don't have a compassionate bone in my body."

Milam looked at his boots. "I'd have to say that was not so."

"Go back in there. Get off my elbow. Drink coffee with Boudinot, I don't care," Mari stated, and started down the stairs. "I've got to think about all of this. Right now, you and Boudinot and this child are complications in my well thought out plans."

Milam smiled. "The nice things about plans is they can change . . . just like people."

"Get away from me." Mari tossed her hand as she descended. "I'm uncommonly tired of men at the moment."

"Yes, ma'am"—Milam corrected himself—"Miss Marshay. She's a real nice child."

"If I had wanted children, I would have had my own."

"Same as a husband, I suspect," Milam spoke to himself as he reëntered the room where Boudinot sat.

"What?" Mari paused on the stairs.

"I said you'd make a good mother."

"I'm not the motherly type."

"Sure you are. You're a woman."

Descending the stairs, Mari muttered to herself. "That twisted logic has ruined many a good woman."

Mari stood on the bottom step with her hand on

the rail, looking at Cricket Dawson playing with a feather. Seeing Mari, the little girl smiled and lifted her arms. "Damn," she said to herself. Mari Marshay, woman of the world, independent woman, gripped the rail for she had fallen that very instant in love.

"Well, ain't you gonna hold her?" asked Louise. She jiggled the little girl. "That high-toned white woman ain't even be polite, is she, sugar?"

"Have you lost your mind, too?" Mari said, walking to the bench where she lifted Cricket from Louise's arms.

"Maybe. Miz Todd was drivin' me crazy. She don't have the least idea how to deal with people of color. And that sheriff. You'd better snap that one up, honey. He come a long way to find you."

"He had to bring the child."

"Oh, he was comin' to you a long time 'fore that."

Mari put her cheek against Cricket's hair. "God in heaven, what am I thinking?"

"You need that man."

"I don't need any man."

"That's just the perfect time to pick a good one."

"I do not need *that* man. He's a local sheriff."

"He quit that when he left Texas. He was a captain with John Bell Hood."

"You've had a lot of time for conversation."

"Oh, he's easy to talk to about the little girl."

"So now he doesn't have a job?"

"Sure he does. He's gonna run that big old ranch on the Brazos for you and Cricket."

Mari looked up at Milam who had reappeared on the banister above.

"Miss Marshay," he began, "I've been thinking."

"Here it comes, honey."

"Shut up, Louise."

"You know that ranch of Tim Dawson's out on the Brazos. Well, that is good land, rich grass, lots of water. Them old cows are standing up to their udders in the prettiest grass. Anyway, I'd like to run it for you. I'm honest. And I have experience. I once had a ranch of my own."

"What happened to your ranch, Mister Milam?" Mari cocked her head, studying the tall, lean lawman coming down the stairs.

"I lost it."

"That's all the recommendation I could want," Mari said dryly.

"It was a bad drought year and the Reconstruction was squeezin' us Texicans pretty hard. It wasn't the stock business I was bad at. I believe I could do better, given another opportunity."

"He's got a Bible with his name in it, a bank-book, and a picture of that old ranch in his gear," Louise whispered.

Mari looked at her with raised eyebrows. "You went through his things?"

Louise smiled and shrugged.

"You're a gambler, aren't you?" ventured Milam.

Mari shook her head. "I gave up gambling, Mister Milam. I'm only interested in sure things."

"Sweet Jesus, this is it," muttered Louise at her elbow.

Milam walked off the final step and stopped in front of Mari.

"Where's Boudinot?" asked Mari.

"He's decided to get his brother out of here and, when he's fully recovered, go to Washington to pursue the case against Kraul."

"I'm disappointed," Mari said idly. "I thought he was sincere in his regard for me."

"Boudinot's all right. He's a square-shooter. Said to tell you to say hello if you ever got to Philadelphia. We settled like gentlemen."

Mari's eyes wandered up to the landing where Boudinot leaned in the open doorway. "I dare not think how."

The woman's and the Indian's eyes met and lingered. Both smiled softly. Finally he waved a small gallant salute.

"We flipped a coin," Milam said. Mari's eyes narrowed on the former sheriff. He smiled, then sobered before her gaze. "It was a trick coin, I'd been savin'."

Mari sighed. She looked at Cricket in her arms. When she looked up at the landing again, Boudinot was gone. She turned and looked about the dismal dépôt at Three Forks. She smiled. "Unemployed, lost his land, cheats at coin tosses." Shaking her head, she walked away toward the open door. "The combination is irresistible," she whispered to herself. Aloud she said: "This is business, Milam. All the arrangements for this child's future have to be worked out."

As she stepped onto the porch platform, Frank Barnes of the McAlester engine tipped his cap to her. "We're goin' back now, miss."

"Do you have room for several passengers?"

Barnes smiled and pointed at the boxcar where Mari's elegant luggage sat. "Yes, ma'am. I figured you might be changing trains."

About the Author

Cynthia Haseloff was born in Vernon, Texas and was named after Cynthia Ann Parker, perhaps the best-known of 19th-Century white female Indian captives. The history and legends of the West were part of her upbringing in Arkansas where her family settled shortly after she was born. She wrote her first novel, *Ride South!*, with the encouragement of her parents. Published in 1980, the back cover of the novel proclaimed Haseloff as "one of today's most striking new Western writers." It is an unusual book with a mother as the protagonist, searching for her children out of love and a sense of responsibility, rather than from a desire for revenge or fame. Haseloff went on to write four more novels in the early 1980s. Two focused on unusual female protagonists. Of the two, *Marauder* was Haseloff's most historical and finest novel among her early books. As one review put it: "*Marauder* has humor and hope and history." It was written to inspire pride in Arkansans, including the students she had known when she taught high school while trying to get her first book published. Haseloff's characters embody the fundamental values—honor, duty, courage, and family—that prevailed on the American frontier and were instilled in the young Haseloff by her own "heroes," her mother and her grandmother. Haseloff's stories, in a sense, dramatize how these values endure when challenged by the adversities and cruelties of frontier existence. Her talent rests in her ability to tell a story with an economy of words and in the seemingly effortless way she uses language. Haseloff, whose previous novels include *The Chains of Sarai Stone*, *Man Without Medicine*, *The Kiowa Verdict*, this last the winner of the WWA Spur Award for Best Western Novel in 1997, and *Satanta's Woman* once said: "I love the West, perhaps not all of its reality, for much of it was cruel and hard, but certainly its dream and hope, and the damned courage of people trying to live within its demands."

Center Point Large Print
600 Brooks Road / PO Box 1
Thorndike ME 04986-0001 USA

(207) 568-3717

US & Canada:
1 800 929-9108
www.centerpointlargeprint.com